Carter, the cabman

Carter,
the cabman

'A reverie'

by Toby Virgo

Illustrated *by* Daniele Serra

LUNE ATTIC PRESS

LUNE ATTIC PRESS

Pickering, North Yorkshire, UK

First published in Great Britain in 2021 by Lune Attic Press

First edition, 2021

Front cover, map and illustrations by Daniele Serra.

A CIP catalogue record for this book is available in the British Library.

ISBN: 978-1-8384873-0-0

Printed and bound by CPI Group (UK) Ltd, Croydon, CR0 4YY.

To Suneil,

It's time to take
a new tour...
this time into the
netherworld
of Victorian London...
enjoy,

Toby

56/250

To Junek,

It's time to take
a new tour ...

this time into the
netherworld
of Victorian London ...

Enjoy,

Toby

'What will you give?'

London: A Selected History, 1600-1888.

1611 **The King James Bible** is published making Christian teaching accessible to all and helping English become the dominant world language.

1665 **The Great Plague** kills 100,000 people, a quarter of London's population.

1666 **The Great Fire** burns for five days destroying five-sixths of the medieval City including 13,200 houses and 87 parish churches.

1667 **Paradise Lost** by John Milton is published.

1701 **Bevis Marks Synagogue** built following the legal return of Jews to England.

1708 **St Paul's Cathedral** completed.

1724 **Jack Sheppard,** notorious pickpocket and jail-breaker is hanged at Tyburn aged 22.

1749 **Bow Street Runners** founded, London's first professional police force.

1780 **The Gordon Riots** spring out of anti-Catholic feeling in London.

1800 **London Population** c. 1 million people.

1807 **Gas-lights** first installed in Pall Mall.

1811 **Ratcliffe Highway Murders** leave seven people dead after two families are attacked in their own homes twelve days apart in the same part of Limehouse.

1834 **Joseph Hansom** of York patents the design for a two-wheeled horse-pulled cabriolet.

1837 **Queen Victoria** becomes monarch of Great Britain and Ireland.

1851   **The Great Exhibition** is visited by over six million people.

1854   **Broad Street Cholera Outbreak** kills six hundred and sixteen people. Its cause is later traced to contaminated drinking water.

1858   **The Great Stink** pervades the capital for three months as a build-up of human waste and industrial effluent poisons the River Thames.

1863   **The Metropolitan Railway** (the world's first underground passenger railway) opens.

1881   **Fenian Bombing Campaign** begins, targeting mainly government, military and police buildings.

1886   **Tower Bridge** under construction.

1887   **Trafalgar Square Riots**

1888   **London Population** c. 5 million people.

1888   **Emma Elizabeth Smith**, a forty-five-year-old woman, is attacked at the junction of Brick Lane and Osborn Street, Whitechapel, in the early hours of April 3rd. Her injuries are so severe that she dies the following day. No-one is ever charged for her murder.

1888   **Martha Tabram**, a thirty-nine-year-old woman, is found stabbed to death on a landing of George Yard Buildings, Whitechapel, on August 7th at 5am. Her assailant is not found.

1888   **Mary Ann Nichols**, a forty-three-year-old woman, is found dead at 3.40am on 31st August, in Buck's Row, Whitechapel. Her throat has been slashed and her body mutilated. Investigations into her killing prove fruitless.

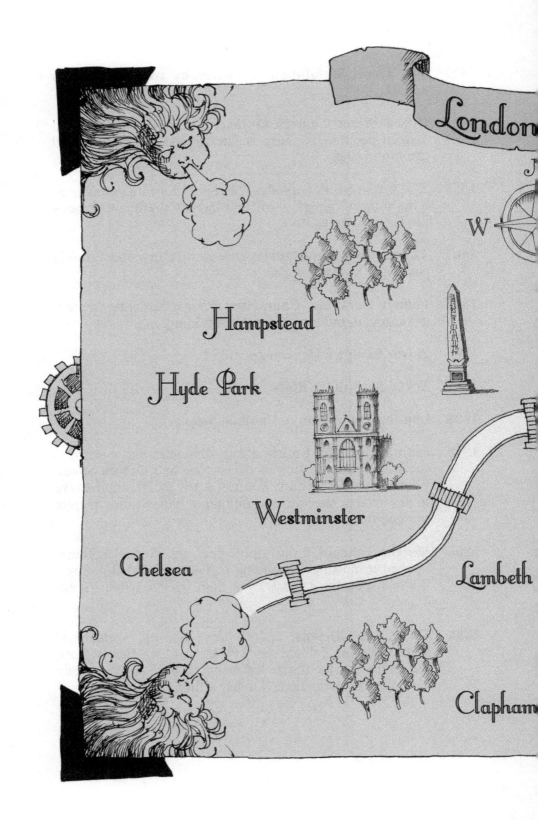

London

W

Hampstead

Hyde Park

Westminster

Chelsea

Lambeth

Clapham

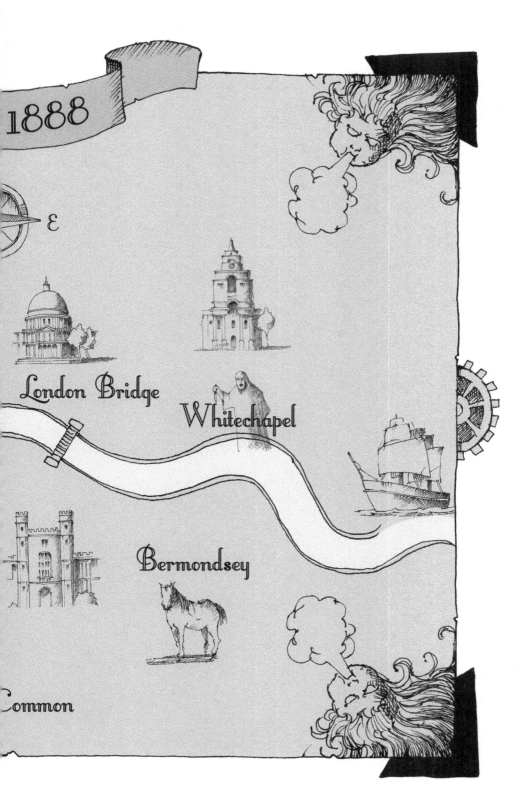

1888

E

London Bridge

Whitechapel

Bermondsey

Common

Preface

*[Note on the origins and ordering of the text by
J. Cripps B.A. (Hons) Hist]*

*

The book you are about to read is not my story – nor is it really my story to tell.

How the text - or I should say the various papers - first came into my possession I will endeavour to explain very shortly, but first please allow me to introduce myself: I am Julian Cripps of *Cripps' ABC (Collectibles) Ltd., Est. 1919.*

My family's modest but enduring enterprise has been based in London's East End for nearly seventy years, moving premises only once to its current location in Whitechapel as a result of the original shop being destroyed in the Blitz, which proved, understandably, to be the death knell for many a small or medium-sized business – yet not, mercifully, for ours. Founded by my grandfather Cornelius Cripps on the crumbs of his War Pension on his return from the trenches of Ypres, *Cripps' ABC* - that is, Antiques, Books and Curios - started life as a one-man mobile operation with old Cornelius hawking various artefacts he had found or acquired to folk in public houses, market squares or anyone else who chanced to encounter him. Enjoying surprising early success, he boldly took out the lease on an empty cobblers in Bishopsgate, soon finding the need to employ an assistant whilst at the same time developing his own expertise so that in scarcely six or seven years he presided over a profitable trade on a now thriving street that came to be known affectionately as 'Peddler's Row'.

Following the catastrophe of the destruction of the original shop my father took on the all-important task of finding new premises, in the end plumping for a shop unit on lowly Brick Lane in part because of its cheaper overheads but also because he rightly sensed that the area's time had come. So it was that the baton of the family name was passed onto me and that, forty years on, I find myself the proud proprietor of the institution that is *Cripps*.

Like most other businesses over the years our operations have had to adapt to survive, evolving in perfect disharmony with the wider rise and fall of the domestic (and increasingly, the global) market. When there is a boom and lots of money to spend our business suffers as the nouveau riche splash their cash on all things new and even the relatively impoverished do not have the pressing need to flog, pawn (or be forcibly parted with) their older, inherited yet valuable things. Conversely, in times of recession a tide of delightful antiques flows our way for which the owner will accept almost any offer, and the white-collar worker's wife grits her teeth and stops to look in our shop window in search of value in places she would never have deigned to step inside a mere two years previously. As we are currently in a time of plenty not many a house clearance reaches my door and I have need to go hunting for the next day's bargain-basement; all the more fortuitous, then, that I should have acted on an impulse to check out the offerings of a fire sale at an old rag-and-bone yard which I spotted as I caught the number 15 home from a very uncomfortable meeting at the bank.

In truth, I arrived well after the event as everything of lasting value had long been hoovered up by those rivals who had got there before me; what little was left represented the real rubbish, the bust and broken of an ill-spent lifetime amassing others people's junk. I scanned with increasingly revolted eyes at the piles of damp comics, the chipped stoneware and china and the ghastly mass-produced 'art', lamenting the meagre cost of a single bus ticket so worthless was the residue. Indeed, I was about to leave before the seller could accost me when a large grey shape shoved in a corner caught my eye.

Moving closer I immediately saw that the dust-covered object was in fact an old Gladstone bag: hardly a rare artefact in my field yet still uncommon enough to be considered a worthy find, its value, as ever, dependant on its condition. Sadly, when I came to wipe away the soil, this particular specimen looked every inch its age, its leather cracked and even pierced in places, one of its handles detached from the main body of the bag and the brass clasps all tarnished and bent. As I tried and failed to pick the lock, he finally caught up with me.

'There's nothing in it. Just a load of dirty rags.'

'How much?'

'Ten.'

I shook my head. 'I'll give you five.'

I waited to hear the air being sucked through his gums. 'Eight. No less. And a bloody steal at that!'

I nodded and allowed myself a smile. 'I'll take it,' I said.

*

For a week or so the bag sat quite unthought-of in a different dusty corner – this time behind the large beech counter of my shop. Trade remained slow - painfully so - and one day my only visitor was my neighbour Rami, owner of *Mistry's Most Authentic Bangladeshi Cuisine* who first asked after my health, then on casting a knowing look around my deserted store reminded me for the third time in as many months, 'Please do not be offended, Mr Julian, but should you ever consider selling your shop…'

I could not be really upset by his charming manner and did not blame him – in the past few years I had borne witness to more than a dozen independents go under or get swallowed up by the powerful new moguls of the exotic food trade with Brick Lane itself changing in front of my very eyes into a street of endless curry houses with more lights than Blackpool Illuminations. Indeed, I was a regular happy patron of several myself and other than its ruinous effect on my waistband could see no reasonable objection for this popular empire's continued meteoric rise. Yet much as I joked with him, telling him that my little shop was old England's last outpost and that I would only leave *Cripps* in an (antique) wooden box, I wondered how much longer I could fend him off and knew that he could sense the turmoil in my soul.

It was a relief, then, at the end of yet another woeful day to suddenly recall my recent acquisition of the Gladstone and after locking up the shop I soon located its lumpen form, lifting it with ease onto the otherwise empty counter with a naïve and childlike joy.

It took several minutes for me to solve the puzzle and prize open the main lock. On realizing I had successfully done so I tried to savour the moment before finally opening the bag and exposing its contents to the fresh air for the first time in who knows how long. A slightly stale odour rose out the carryall – other than that, the interior appeared very well-preserved, remarkably so in fact given the parlous state of the outer leather. It was, just like I had been told, stuffed full of dirty old rags and balls of screwed-up paper, doubtless to thwart the moths. No hidden treasure here, then, I told myself.

Picking out the crumpled-up sheets and the stained squares of material, I delved deeper – to my surprise laying my hand on the stiff, unyielding corners of some kind of hardback book. Lifting it out as carefully as I could, the spine still gave way in my hand, its many yellowed pages taking spontaneous flight and scattering in all directions over the hundreds of ornaments, ordered bric-a-brac and more choice objets d'art that populated the shop floor. Now down on my hands and knees as I peered under the display cabinets, I dutifully recovered them all, in the process also finding a trove of loose change, a lost invoice and the furred remains of what might once have been a cheese ploughman's roll. Clutching onto at least thirty pieces of paper, I set the mess down on the counter under my heavy Bakelite phone along with the shell of the original book which I now knew to be an old diary or journal.

Returning to the bag, I saw that the book itself had been resting upon a neatly-folded newspaper cutting, dated Saturday 22nd September, 1888. At least, I thought, there could be no real debate about its exact time period as I tried to gather a few more clues about its provenance. All that was left inside though was a rusted old horseshoe and a length of broken metal that may have come from a medical instrument or possibly a workman's knife.

I sighed: I understood that in essence what I had bought was a mediocre item which I would have to work hard on in order to make my margin, in addition to a likely worthless journal, leaving me in a moral fix over whether I ought to spend the dead time required to restore it to its original state. The rag-and-bone man, I winced, had really seen me coming.

Leaving everything on the counter, this was a job that could be put off until tomorrow.

*

I arrived back at the shop the following morning in a much more positive frame of mind.

As I turned on the lights, opened the blinds and unlocked the shop door, the old Gladstone on the counter seemed to me like a much more attractive proposition. After all, I reflected, I had not bought it without thinking and had adhered as always to the three golden questions my late father had insisted I pose of any object:

What is it, who would buy it and why?

As to the 'What?' you may think we have already dealt with that question but I can assure you we have not. The 'What?' actually refers to the 'ABC' part of our name against which fixed standard every item must be judged. 'A' as you know is for 'antique', and the old bag just about qualified, an antique - as well as being a thing of aesthetic or historical significance - often also defined as an object of at least one hundred years old. With the newspaper cutting handily present to help date it, it seemed that the Gladstone was bang on the limit. Next, 'B' for book – obviously not. Yet I thought of the decrepit memoir I'd salvaged from its depths and my day's impending task of trying to restore it. Who knows, I fantasized, what it might be? Finally, 'C' for curio. Most certainly here, and with a quirky tale waiting to be spun around it, its list value might be bumped up by two times or more. All in all then, for the 'What?' part the bag fit the bill.

Moving on to the 'Who?': who would buy such an object? I'd instinctively leaned toward the international market visualising a snap-happy American or Japanese tourist still high from the previous night's Ripper tour and still smelling of sushi or the mixed-meat kebab they'd devoured with relish at its conclusion. Now all they required was an authentic souvenir to pass around the office or show off to their friends as proof they had walked in the footsteps of history and seen the 'real' London.

Finally, 'Why?' To use? Likely not, for it would not be economical to pay for the bag to be professionally repaired. Possibly, then, as a storytelling prop or an item for fancy dress? Or, in the absence of a clinching reason why, perhaps I could concoct one?

How to do it? The way all the good storytellers did – through a heady cocktail of truth and intrigue: a Gladstone bag, owner unknown, complete with crumbling journal. 'What do you know, sir, about that Autumn of Terror?...'

I now felt a whole lot better about my purchase which I'd hardly paid a king's ransom for anyway. My father had taught me well and as long as I stuck to his rules I'd rarely fail to at least recoup my investment.

Profit, however, was the least thing on my mind as I sat down and started to leaf through the pile of papers I had so successfully disarranged like a pack of playing cards. I idly pulled one out and began to read through its contents, within just a few sentences finding myself drawn deep into the scribe's world, hooked by his story and challenged by his rugged dogma until I reached the last line and returned to the pile to make an anxious search for the following page. The black ink set down long ago on cheap paper veered between a neat, regular block-print and the mad scratchings of a man possessed whose pen could hardly keep up with his outpourings, so contrasting that the scripts could almost be the work of two different hands. Yet once I had learned to decipher his writing and had re-ordered the opening pages, I realized that what I'd inadvertently stumbled across was no mere layman's chronicles but the visionary discourses of a prophet: part diary, part family history, part confessional; part prose-poem and all wild, religious reverie, the dog-eared papers amounted to no less than a full-frontal assault on the Age, punctuated by outbursts of love, loss and all too human pain.

I sat quite engrossed in my swivel chair as I pored over the extraordinary document, the minutes turning into hours until I was ripped from the fog of Victorian London back into the dazzling August sunlight of modern-day Whitechapel by the tinkling of the doorbell. As I looked up, the silhouette of a tall, heavy man lingered at the threshold before stepping into the shop and as my eyes readjusted one of the working grandfather clocks told me that it was already a quarter-to-twelve.

'Good morning, sir!'

My first customer of the day declined to greet me, instead slowly and silently stalking the merchandise, the type who are afraid to ask questions lest they be committed to a sale, and as he shuffled forward I could hear his laboured breathing as his huge bulk filled the aisle, threatening the breakables.

I noted his new 'London Dungeon' baseball cap, his lumberjack shirt and khaki shorts over which his gut freely spilled like the year's first ice-melt at Niagara, his unalluring look perfectly set-off by sandals over socks which left an imprint of sweat wherever they stepped. After a good ten minutes of this performance my patience began to wear thin – at which point he glanced over at the counter and his shiny face lit-up at the sight of the Gladstone.

'What is that?' he bluntly asked me, in the expected accent.

'Oh, it's just an old bag sir,' I replied.

'Just an old bag! Gee, I bet it's older than some of New Jersey's cities! I'd like to examine it if I may?'

'Erm, I'm afraid…it's not for sale.'

'Now come on!'

'I'm sorry sir. If it's a bag that you're looking for –'

'I'm only interested in that one.'

'I'm sorry.'

'It's one of those doctor's bags, isn't it? Our guide told us about them yesterday. What are they called now?…'

'It's called a Gladstone.'

'That's the one! Gladstone bags. Named after the British Prime Minister. Some believe they were the type used by –'

'Jack the Ripper,' I nodded wearily.

'Right! Now you're talking. May I ask how old it is?'

'I think it may be from around that time.'

'From 1888! Are you serious? Can I touch it?'

'No.'

'I'll give you fifty dollars for it.'

'I'm sorry sir.'

'A hundred dollars then!'

'I'm really sorry, sir, but it's not for –'

'What's wrong with you Brits?' he exploded. 'Don't you understand money? I'm a customer right here in your goddamn shop - right now, the only customer if you haven't noticed - making you a straight-up offer for a piece of trash and you've the nerve to treat me like this? Little wonder your shop is empty! Good day to you, dear sir!'

He turned and stormed out as quickly as a fat man could. I, for my part, remained for a few moments in my chair, eventually rising to my feet, walking to the door, flipping the opening hours sign to 'Closed For Lunch' and turning the key.

I felt foolish: despite his unpleasantness I knew that the man had been justified in his rage and that I'd have to wait a very long time to receive another offer even close to the one he'd made. Did the bag have such an absurd hold over me already?

It took most of the afternoon for me to organize the rest of the papers and I stayed late into the evening so that I might finish reading the journal, making notes on several puzzling or disconcerting passages and other points I wished to follow up. Man, however, cannot live off inspiration alone, and when the full neon of Brick Lane had announced the arrival of night proper I called it a day to go in search of a different kind of nourishment.

I headed north for no reason in particular, peering through the windows of *The Shy Tiger, Naan Better, The Khyber Pass* and *Balti Towers,* all far too busy for a lone middle-aged man to feel comfortable in as he tucked into his aloo gobi. I soon turned back as I tired of being harassed by beaming front-of-house staff working hard to entice the drunken walk-in trade, retracing my steps past my shuttered shop and inevitably ending up inside *Mistry's* which at least had a choice of tables and a menu I knew too well.

It did not take long for Rami to notice my arrival and as he brought a pickle tray and three papadums to my table he had a twinkle in his eye.

'Ah! Mr Julian: good evening! You have come to open negotiations for your shop?'

'No Rami. I've come for a bloody good feed.'

'No problem,' he chuckled. 'We can leave that until later. Shall I get you a drink whilst you decide what you want?'

'I'd like a drink, yes, but I already know what I fancy.'

'I cannot interest you in any of tonight's specials?'

I pulled a face and shook my head.

'May I ask why?'

'Because a maître d' once told me that specials were all the stuff that was about to go off.'

'I see. In that case, please allow me to guess: to start perhaps a channa puri; then for your main either a saag paneer or else I ask chef to make your chosen bhuna with a side of aloo gobi and pilau rice. To finish – no...maybe not today. How did I do?'

'Very well. You forgot about my drink though.'

'I think not. My colleague is already on his way...' and with that a waiter holding a silver tray placed my desired pint in front of me.'

'You are a magician Rami. I should never have doubted you. Channa puri and king prawn bhuna it is.'

'A good choice Mr Julian! Enjoy your food.'

'Thank you,' I smiled. 'I will.'

Enjoy it I certainly did after the morning's mini-drama and the day's detective work – but brain work is hungry work and in spite of the abundance of mouthwatering fare by the time my stomach had been defeated my gut was still unsatisfied as my mind turned again to the problem of the book.

'Would you like to see the dessert menu?' my friend asked me.

I held up my hands. 'Thank you – but I'm stuffed.'

'Did you enjoy it?'

'Always, Rami, always.'

'Excellent! I'm glad. If you will forgive me though, Mr Julian, you do not quite seem your normal self.'

And so I decided to tell him about the saga of the bag.

'It's hard for me to put my finger on it,' I concluded, after relaying the story you yourself have now heard, 'but I can't help but feel that something is missing.'

'Hmm. Are you sure you still have all the pages of the diary?'

'I'm pretty certain, yes. There are no obvious gaps and the dates seem to correspond.'

'Have you double-checked the bag? What about its contents?'

'There's not a lot to check.'

'Nevertheless, I would suggest doing so again. My uncle used to say that when you have a problem the answer is usually under your nose.'

It was good of him to help but I held out little faith – what could I possibly hope to find that I hadn't already? I settled my bill, shaking Rami's hand and exiting *Mistry's* with a mumbled (if insincere) promise to give more thought to his ongoing interest in the shop, stepping onto Brick Lane to be hit for six by the raw chill of an August night under London's cloudless sky. My shock at the depth of the summer cold was only magnified by the sight of a homeless girl curled up in the doorway opposite. Perhaps fourteen or fifteen years old at a push her plight was a sobering sight, yet one, I regret to say, that I was getting increasingly used to in our supposedly more enlightened times. My own way home involved a half-an-hour walk or else a wait for the night bus as a cab was a luxury I couldn't currently afford. Feeling woozy, I checked my pockets for my house keys and debated what to do. Unlike the poor girl or the legion of Unfortunates referred to in the Gladstone's journal, I did not have to long endure the sudden drop in temperature or be exposed to the many dangers and privations of a night spent out on the streets. I looked round at the darkened façade of *Cripps:* it wouldn't be the first time I'd resorted to sleeping in the shop.

Loud wolf whistles, football chants and yells that grew nearer made my decision for me; I lifted the shutter, unlocked the door and deactivated the alarm, hastily closing up behind me. Switching on the main lights I made straight for the storeroom where I kept a camping mat and a sleeping bag for just such an occasion; finding them, I moved over to the narrow space behind the counter and rolled them out on the floor. The seventies parquet was still littered with the balls of paper I'd pulled out of the bag and neglected to tidy up. I started to fling them in the bin when I remembered Rami's advice, on a whim picking one up and flattening it out, to my delight finding that the crumpled page was adorned with the same careful handwriting that also graced the earlier sections of the diary.

I checked another: that too was filled with his words, and soon I had recovered a small ream of discarded folios, some pristine, others damaged by exposure to damp and cold but all the work of the same hand on a finer grade of paper and manifestly written in a phase of life quite apart from that of the events recorded in the diary. I sat down and started to read, breaking only for a few minutes to make strong coffee when I knew I was there for the long haul; very soon it became clear that *these* were the episodes from the past that the journal had referred to so obliquely, representing the missing pieces of the jigsaw and set down in ink only after long and pained reflection before being deemed inadequate, put to one side in grief or shame – or stowed away in the Gladstone and gifted to posterity. Irrespective of the scribe's own wishes or intentions, by the time morning had arrived I knew I'd been made the steward of a lost history that needed to be told.

For this task it was clear that the easiest option would be to place the journal and all of the manuscripts in the hands of a suitable publisher, allowing me to sit back and let them do the hard work whilst insisting that my name appear prominently on the cover and I get credit (and welcome publicity) for my scholarly instinct and once-in-a-lifetime find. Yet the more I pondered it the more I knew I could not trust any of them not to pull it apart, wilfully misconstrue it or give into the temptation to sensationalize the whole thing in search of a quick and easy buck – not least because all of the diary's entries related to the evening of Friday 7th September, 1888 and the early morning of Saturday 8th: an infamous night even on London's storied stage and one which was to give birth to a legend. I rebelled at the idea and resolved to do what he who'd written it never had the chance to during his own lifetime: I would publish it myself and almost certainly be damned.

Here, my own historical training served to help me as I soon realized that the various excerpts would clearly lose something if artificially rendered into a pure diary – and yet equally make no sense if what dated entries that still existed were simply followed by the jumbled screed I'd recovered from the floor. The best solution, I decided, was to make it a man's testimony: personal, hard to take and with all the aura of a bad dream but in its own small way as potent a rebuke as Luther's *Ninety-Five Theses* nailed to a church door. This I think I achieved, arranging the separate entries how I thought best and in a way that made sense to me, after a few weeks managing to produce a readable book complete with chapter titles (inevitably of my own choosing).

In the course of all this the possibility suddenly occurred to me that the journal might be a fake, planted in the bag and left in the reclamation yard to be miraculously 'discovered' by an unwitting actor such as I many years after the dark days referred to within that continue to exercise such fascination today; indeed, several points suggested so. Not least of these is the author's own prose, a bit too articulate some might say for a working man of the time who would have had little of what we call a proper schooling. The argument is a reasonable one but just as there is nothing standard about the past nor is there about this book or its author. We do our forebears a disservice to consider them all the same and what is history anyway but modern prejudice: distilled, refined a little and made more palatable for our tastes, but prejudice nonetheless.

His voice is what it is: that of a man raised on the good King James in the era when new faces inhabited the capital and Empire still strived to order all before (in the words of a well-known poem) the world went all awry. Perhaps that process started with this journal. In the end, you will be the judge of its authenticity.

Here it is then, warts and all, presented for your enjoyment and perhaps your education. I have included a short chronology of London to lend some historical context for those not familiar with the time. I have also included a copy of the newspaper article found inside the bag. Beyond that, the words are his: he, who I have never met, will never meet and yet feel I know; a man whose thoughts live again after a century and who I now have the honour to introduce to you as Carter, the cabman.

Julian Cripps,
London, October 1988.

Whitechapel Horror: Verdict of MURDER

The jury in the case of the Whitechapel Horror returned a verdict of murder in court this afternoon.

In his full summing up on the last day of the inquest following three weeks of evidence, the Coroner, Mr Wynne Baxter, recalled to the minds of the twelve men all the known facts relating to the dead woman and other relevant points of the case, reminding them of her intemperate and irregular habits, of her state of great intoxication during her final hours and of the discovery of her mutilated body by a passing carman at approximately 3.40 am on Friday August 31st.

Her disarrayed clothing had at first suggested that she had been outraged but this had proved not to be so and it had taken the police doctor little time to ascertain that she had been killed by savage cuts to the throat and abdomen made by a strong-bladed instrument and had most likely been attacked where she fell, her assailant surely carrying the marks of her blood upon his person yet somehow escaping unnoticed from Buck's Row before merging into the early morning traffic.

It was, the Coroner stated, impossible to ignore that this was one of four similar deaths in the local vicinity currently being investigated, the latest having occurred in the period since this inquest had been commenced – now in the hands of another jury. All have taken place in the hours after midnight in places of public resort, all were middle-aged women, all married but living apart from their husbands.

As to motive, robbery was out of the question, all four being destitute themselves; jealousy could not altogether be ruled out, though there is nothing in any case to prove or suggest it; in the absence of all else, then, it could only be surmised that each frenzied attack be the product of a hitherto unimagined strain of lunacy, all the more disturbing with the growing realization that those responsible must still be at large.

In the light of such advice it took the jury twenty minutes to deliver their verdict:

'Wilful murder against some person or persons unknown.'

Carter,
the cabman

Chapters

1

The Grey Mares of Bermondsey

AS DARKNESS FALLS and I hurry through the streets of London, I think little of the trials of the night ahead, eager only to be reunited with my beloved Belle.

Entering the yard, I check first that she has been fed and watered, collecting bridle and reins before slipping through the stable door and delighting in lurking until she suddenly lifts her head from the trough, snorting loudly in recognition as she catches my scent and nuzzles into my outstretched arm.

She is one of threescore currently stabled here and there has been livery of sorts in this part of Bermondsey for over a hundred years. They say there are nigh on fifteen thousand horses now working the city streets and I can well believe it – but none, I'll wager, can hold a torch to my beautiful Belle, her silvery mane and grey mare's tail a glimmer of hope in the gloom like a dart shot across my waking dreams. In fact, since I switched to working the twilight hours, I josh that this faithful old charge is now my night mare, sent by Providence and the Lord above to keep me from straying in the London fog.

My name, by the way, is Jeremiah Carter, and as my title suggests I come from a line of pious horsemen. My father, Joseph, was a night-soilman, his own father a groom, both hale and God-fearing men who preached the ills of the bottle so that from a babe-in-arms I was steeped only in the Psalms and horsey lore, the world as I knew it measured strictly in hands. This spot south of the river has been home to Carters since time immemorial: legend has it that our family name was first mentioned in the Domesday survey of the Hundred of Brixton and it is a matter of historical record that our people have lived and worked in various parts of Southwark in the centuries ever since, here

1

even in those halcyon days when the area was little more than a few enclosed fields dotted with the occasional farmstead and when the name 'Carter' accounted for one in seven of the local population, as common as sour hay at Candlemas.

Today, my ancestors would hardly know their own lands, the birch groves and stands of alder long hacked down, the rolling pastures crudely paved over and replaced by regimented rows of red brick houses, noisy workshops, dirty factories and busy yards, so that it is now possible to ride for several minutes without seeing a flower or tree. So much, then, for 'progress' and the wisdom of man. Yet how the grey horse came to bide on what was once just a high point in a patch of marshy ground is an altogether simpler, if grimmer, tale.

Chosen for their colour by the Scots Dragoons in their task of keeping order amongst the clans of the Borders, the greys got their first taste of London during the time of the Glorious Revolution, the regiment itself coming to be known as the Royal Scots Greys before being sent back home for further duties. Then came that immortal year - all hail 1815! - as news reached us of Napoleon's escape from Elba and it seemed that overnight the British Army doubled in size and the Greys soon numbered a thousand officers and men! Most needed fresh mounts and with little time to find them the net was cast far and wide so that no farm or smallholding missed the call. Torn from their homes and at the mercy of strange new masters, all reached the Channel exhausted after long days of hard riding only to be sent straight on to the Continent and the horrors of war. Just four troops' worth remained in England, many lame from their journeys, held back for a second wave that history tells us never came.

Of Waterloo and its peerless glories I need not regale you; enough that all recall the deeds of the Ensign Ewart who led the charge and wrested the French Eagle from the very hand of its standard-bearer – but who, I wonder, spares a care for the grey who bravely bore him and the hundreds more - hapless cannon fodder - that never left the field of war? To think that the sires of Belle were next in line for such slaughter! Yet in hindsight perhaps it may have been better so: for the lucky few that had cheated death in the mud and slime, their tribulations had only just begun.

Sold off as Crown property to the highest bidder, the worst cases went to the knacker's yard, four-hoofed heroes tossed aside like so much surplus munitions. The best specimens returned to the life of the plough where a common lot of toil and ceaseless drudgery awaited...but the biggest number found themselves drawn as if by invisible reins into the tumult of the capital so that the grey horse, wild spirit of the machair, found a new abode in the beating heart of the Empire on which the sun never sets. Bought by Silas George, the famed horse trader, he schooled them hard for the difficult road ahead, turning wilful beasts reared on rich upland grasses into pliant machines that ran on thin air and were good for a dozen tasks. Pack horses, cart horses, carriages and coaches, the greys were soon a familiar sight on every street corner and the joy of every urchin from Camberwell to Crouch End.

Their arrival heralded an explosion in the use of horse-drawn transport – culminating in the coming of the hansom cab. Faster, cheaper and light enough as to only require a single steed, the hansoms replaced the hackney carriage as the chief vehicle for hire and in one fell swoop the greys had found their true calling. Hardy yet surprisingly nimble, their smaller frames were tailor-made for weaving through the choked highways at breakneck speed, many finding a place here in Peter's Yard which quickly established itself as one of the busiest cab offices in the Borough. The mares in particular were prized, being found to be more biddable, the headstrong stallions tending to be set aside for heavier work so that every cab driver's heart lifted at the sight of a favourite mare returning to the sanctuary of the yard, breath steaming and clarted from foot to forelock with grime but with her day's work done and a manic glint in the eye. Even now I well remember how father admonished me when I hit out at one in temper as a lad: 'Never forget son,' he growled, 'how they served us – and that they served us well!'

*

3

I obtained my first cab licence aged sixteen, already so well-acquainted with the labyrinth of lanes and alleyways that I was given free rein, so to speak, to properly learn my trade. Within three years I had graduated so far as to take a part share in a private cab so that by the time that I married, aged twenty-two, I had paid all of my dues, was the marvel of my family, master of my own universe and beholden to none. In thrall of it all as all at once my future seemed rosy and my fortune made, there was but one dissenting voice: for father, my luck had come too quick and too easy, and just as he perched restlessly by his wife's side as he bore witness to my every triumph in the last blessed years of his dotage, I thank the Lord he did not live to see my fall, for sure enough the tables turned and his worst fears came back to haunt me as one midwinter's night I lost everything I held dear.

Little that is good can I tell you of the weeks and months that followed; suffice to say that I tumbled headfirst down the darkest rabbit hole where forgetfulness is sold by the hour and from which better men than I have not returned, coming up for air to rail against my Maker and curse the day that I was born. Thus it would have gone on - to what end, I can easily guess - but for a chance encounter with the last living soul the closest thing I had left to kin. Stepping out one early morning from a hostelry, I collided with a passer-by; about to share a few choice words with the stranger, I heard a voice proclaim my name…and from the pit of my despair I made out a familiar shape wreathed in the clinging yellow fog: Father Damien Patrick Cronin.

My boyhood priest - and thus to me the living embodiment of God - I had come to know Him as a being with hairy ears who had dwelt forever in the dappled light of St Mary Magdalen Church. Small in stature, but not of soul, and prone to preach of fire and brimstone to suit the flame-red tinge of his unruly Celtic hair, the Irish Father had been a fixture in Bermondsey so long that it was said he had been put in with the bricks. I had last seen him at the altar – on the day I wed; not long after, he disappeared and I heard a rumour he had urgent ministry to attend to in the docks at Rotherhithe. This news troubled me and his absence marked a break in my habit of devout weekly worship. Distracted by trifles and the mores of marriage, I forgot all about the Sunday lesson and in wholly different ways our two streams diverged from the main current of Christian life.

Later, I learned that having somehow got wind of my troubles he had tasked himself with tracking me down, keeping an ever-watchful eye on his parish rounds until the day of our fateful collision. On that bitter dawn I'd fairly withered under his benevolent gaze but he cajoled me gently like a swineherd with his drift, handling me with unwarranted kindness and fixing a time and place where we could justly parley. Still raw with grief, I kept neither the first nor the second of those appointments and he must have deemed me a lost cause...but on the third chance a fit of conscience befell me and I found him waiting for me like a loyal dog at the prescribed meeting place, sat by the fire in the snug of The Lettered Board – the night, as I see it, when I came in from the cold.

Kicking off my boots and taking up his offer of a medicinal whisky whilst noticing that he himself abstained, I was in no fit state to now recall all that may have been said; what I do know is that I hearkened more than I spoke, and that, lulled by his soft Limerick lilt, I began to thaw a little and rediscover something of my former self, a character as distant and detached from me as the cast of a minor bible story. Perhaps it was all part of Father Cronin's plan to not use that night to invoke the Holy Book. Indeed, in marked contrast with our previous meeting, I got my first real impression of a man whose faith had been sorely tried and the Father seemed to me more purely saintly - and alone - than ever I had known him. Yet as we parted we shook hands and embraced as friends and promised to meet again.

So was to begin a weekly conclave in that secret back room, the rickety bar stools our pews, the wharfside tavern our low cathedral. Having lost my livelihood and now a rare visitor to my own home, the empty hours of day weighed heavy on my soul, lending a special meaning to our regular meetings. The talk - at least at first - was of everything but that of importance, the worst gossip and the idle chaff of the day. Swiftly though, as we became at ease again in each other's company, the conversation turned to deeper matters, and, naturally enough, to the teachings of the Bible, starting with the Psalms.

The bread and water of my youth, just hearing the simple songs of praise was akin to being reunited with lost friends as I found to my joy that, despite my lapse, I could recount most by heart like the best-loved of fairy stories. Our readings began with 'The Lord is my Shepherd':

'The Lord is my shepherd,
I shall not want.
He makes me lie down in green pastures
And leads me to still waters.
He restores my soul:
He leads me in the paths of righteousness
for his name's sake.'

To be led, the Father counselled, a man first needs to accept that he is lost – but to restore a man's soul means to set his spiritual stall in order; to do this he needs to relinquish full control of the reins and accept that, aided by a higher power, he will steer a better path if he unflinchingly and unquestioningly takes the Lord's direction and acts in His name forevermore. Then, upon being led toward Heaven in everything he does, a man himself can be a shepherd.

'For now, you are still a lamb, Jeremiah,' he told me, 'but you too can become a prophet, God's guide by earthly proxy, bringing His Word to the streets of His downtrodden people and showing them the way.'

In such a vein we continued, the season ripening and the year turning from '87 to '88, from sharp November nights - the mast of an Oriental barque looming large against a starlit sky - to malevolent March mists that stole in like a thief across the water and smothered even the Thames' beckoning depths. A few weeks into our study though the focus started to shift and we lingered longer over presages of judgement and doom. Whilst I clamoured

6

to hear more about the Lord's everlasting love, the Father marched us ever on into the valley of shadow, quoting often from the Book of Revelations. Thus we greeted the spring having reached an impasse, the wavering priest and the zealous apostate; it was much to my surprise, then, one night when he suggested that we try a different type of verse:

> *'Long is the way and hard,*
> *that out of Hell leads up to light.'*

What a golden evening this was for me!

In the music of the Psalms the Father had found a way to coax me back into the fold – but in the purity of these lines he had held up a mirror to the struggles of my very own soul! It was only now, awoken by this strange account of the Fall of Man, that I truly came back under God's spell. Each week as the priest motioned to shut the great tome, I leapt to my feet and beseeched him, 'Read me more!', so that I felt my fervour catch and breathe new life into the old man as together we burned the midnight oil. Filled with a longing to learn more and to do the Lord's work, I eventually found the courage to recite a passage on my own; so that whilst I always say that it was my dear grandfather - God rest his soul! - who learned me my letters, it was Brother Damien who taught me how to read.

By the spit and crackle of firelight did we study in earnest: filling our sails, we descried new lands and scaled smoky peaks, beholding iron-clad Giants with 'death-shot glowing' in their hands. We followed Ulysses out of Ithaca, met damsels with dulcimers and relived our youth in the dream of Ossian's hunter on the hill of the heath. Here another Poet took up the mantle, leading us through the three realms of the dead, showing us the shape of the afterlife's path, its cardinal virtues, deadly sins and poetic justice on a soul's journey to God. We read of martyrs who went mad and revolutionaries without arms given the keys to the Golden City; we met Shades, condemned men and creatures never poisoned by sin, allowed a momentary glimpse of the meaning of Eternity as one

7

volume closed and another opened, a mystical trip into a promised land of plenty 'in which it seemed always afternoon'.

Yet all the talk of fresh pastures and a paradise lost also served to turn my thoughts another way: ready to hide no more, I dreamed of horses again and so swallowed my pride to pay a visit to the Yard. Given short shrift by the men, I appealed to their humanity and begged that they at least retain my name. A while later, a message reached me from the firm that the gaffer was short of drivers and had granted me a hearing. He dealt with me tersely and freely admitted that he had only made contact to get himself out of a fix: there had been some disquiet amongst the men - doubtless it would soon die down - that had started to affect even the mares. As such, he was giving me the chance of paid work on the strict condition that I took whatever he offered and on the understanding that I was being handed a week's trial. Delighted, I accepted and he immediately informed me that I would be working the hated curfew shift, 'from the Kings Road to within the sound of St Mary-le-Bow, starting daily at sundown and refusing no fare until dawn.' Watching keenly for my reaction, I simply nodded and thanked him, promising that I would give him no cause to regret his bargain, quickly adding, 'I do though, sir, have one small favour to ask...'

Looking back, I see that I paid no notice to his veiled warnings, bent as I was on setting things right and seizing my chance. I fairly sailed into The Lettered Board on the occasion of our next meeting and Father Cronin seemed pleased with - if a bit uneasy at - my news.

'Take this,' he urged me, pressing a dog-eared volume into my hands, 'and keep it with you, pray each day to the saints and mind to always do His bidding. For God so loved the world that He gave His only son...'

At this, I scarce suppressed a laugh at the way the priest spoke – for it was as if I were to be sacrificed before the heavenly hosts and that it was he who was giving me up. Truth be told, it was a relief to finally strike out on my own again and if I had gone to him needing saving then surely now I had been saved? Another of God's creatures needed saving too and on my first night back I asked around for my beloved mare, finding her in the end tied up and alone in a cold corner of the yard. She heeded me not, so I whispered to her and scratched her ears, all the while noticing that, if not exactly neglected, she appeared thin, unkempt and unloved. Her new owner - a boss-eyed lad who reeked of ale - came to hear me out, as the gaffer and I had agreed, and, somewhat perplexed, jumped at my more than generous offer to take 'the old nag' off his hands. As she had been rested for the day I filled her nosebag with her favourite mix, and she whinnied with joy as I rubbed her down and combed her mane and in no time at all she was quite a different animal, and Belle and I were back together again on Bermondsey's byways as if we had never been apart.

So it is that as the light fades and I strap her to the hansom Belle assents without a murmur, and we prepare once more to tread the streets of my forebears where so many have dared to dream. I blush to say that I also now fancy myself as something of a Poet, so that I can avow, as Milton did, 'What hath night to do with sleep?', adding, like Miranda, as I see Belle champ and toss her noble head:

'I would not wish any companion in the world but you.'

I had thought for a time, during those long winter months, of joining the priesthood – until I realised that the Lord had a different plan. There are those out there who tonight will need me: the weary, the wretched and the lost. His work can be done in a hundred different ways and when all is said, I am just a jarvey for hire: cab number 2704, a cog in the wheel of a monstrous machine and right happy to remain so!

As the gates to Peter's Yard swing open and we set out on our way you may care little for us – but as the fog creeps in and London darkens who can say what trials the hours will bring? Then, I, Jeremiah, may find myself suddenly in demand and in a moment all and sundry flock to my church and the prophet can call himself king. A stray penny for the ferryman will no longer suffice

9

and in the city of dreadful night you may yet cry out to me for mercy.

How much I levy depends on the road you wish to take and what you are prepared to give.

2

Mother Thames

It takes an age for the hansom to push its way onto Bermondsey New Road, besieged as we are by the throng of hawkers, loafers and hangers-on that typically gather at the entrances of most large commercial establishments. Wary of injuring any of the crowd, I loudly turn down all offers of laces, matches, brass polish and lucky charms, thankful to have a mare with such a tolerant nature until at last another drag follows in our wake and the disgruntled mob descends upon a new victim.

Heading south, within a hundred yards we have our first fare and we soon swap the congested streets and constant rumble of sack barrows for the green lanes of West Norwood and the sleepy villas of Sydenham. The long canter-out also provides a perfect start to our evening, allowing me to keep close watch on the progress of Belle: having done so well in the first few weeks of our new partnership, I have since noticed that she is prone to get a little footsore, more than once having to pull up at the roadside whilst in conveyance of a passenger. To date no harm has been done but not all patrons are so forgiving and it only takes one complaint about a lame horse before the beginning of the end is nigh. Having had the farrier out and all her hoofs re-shod there is nothing more I can do. Even at such an hour, the September heat is still oppressive so I cast about for the nearest stream or a local pond. Here, though, the grand private residences revolve around the equine race and it is not far before we find a pile of muddy carrots and a conveniently stationed bucket.

As I wait for Belle I hear footsteps rapidly approaching and a voice calling out: 'Sir! I say, sir! Are you engaged?'

I turn to see a portly, middle-aged, well-dressed man, breathless from his exertions. He mops his brow with a spotted handkerchief and under his arm he carries a leather-bound book and a sheaf of fluttering papers.

'No sir. I am free,' I answer.

'In which direction do you go?' he asks.

'I was about to return into town sir – but I can go almost anywhere you please.'

'I head to Chelsea, if that is convenient?'

'Very good sir. You are just within my limits. Hop on board and we will be off in a jiffy.'

But at my invitation he surprises me, shaking his head and ruefully prodding his hefty pile.

'I have been inspecting licences all day long – it would not do to engage a hansom until I had done the same thing. *The Echo* would have a field day.'

'You'll need to wait then sir,' I mutter, caught off-guard by his request, 'and I'll show you my credentials. I'm sure I have everything you need.'

It takes a minute or so but I locate my papers and hand them over to him, who studies them with ostentatious care.

'You have not been a cab driver long, Mr Carter.'

'Just back two months now sir. Before that, ten years.'

'You were not, I take it, ever detained at Her Majesty's pleasure?'

'No sir.'

'Or otherwise bound over for the Peace?'

'No sir. I was ill.'

'I see. These are long hours that you work and a big area to cover. Is it always at night-time that you ride?'

'Yes sir. It's all the Office had.'

He grunts. 'And your rates: what do you charge?'

'One shilling the first two miles – 3d thereafter. And no man can say fairer than that.'

'No man indeed,' he replies, swinging himself into the seat with a knowing smirk. 'For now, at least, that is...'

A pair of blackbirds call to each other from a hawthorn bush and

I pray Belle does not let me down. I whisper a word of encouragement, untie her from the gate and a quick shake of the ribbons soon sees us away.

I am at the western extremities of my beat here, a world that is not my own.

As we cross the wild common our way is lit only by the stars and the distant radiance from a solitary lodge house and it is hard to believe that we are still in London. This is territory that long ago would have been familiar to a Carter, some of whom would have been retained as stable boys or grooms. How different their lives would have been from mine! Not for them the freedom of the road, the fleeting meetings, the unknown adventure of each new shift; instead, the fixed pattern of day, the set timetable in the same block, in the same stable with the same horses and the same men, before retiring once again to the same food served up on the same plates on the same table in the same room in the same loved and hated tied-cottage. How their minds would have quailed at a life like mine – my landmarks: the Tower, London Bridge, the fish market, the perilous intersection of traffic at Piccadilly; their way-marks: a gap in a fence, a muddy corner by a patch of gorse, the old estate yew that no longer buds. How poorly, too, would I have fared in their miniature worlds and I am consumed by guilt for not having done better in mine.

Still, I feel a sort of connection to these distant men, inheriting, as I have, some of their skills – and in a few cases, their things. My whip, for example (though it is seldom employed) is embossed on its base with an illustrious crest. Some of the prized family heirlooms are the personal effects of one A. Carter, a former head coachman of a well-known Dulwich house, and my father, thinking it still of use, taught me to navigate by the constellations, a foresight for which I have much reason to be grateful tonight. The truth is that life is not always fair and I owe it to my ancestors to see this as my second coming – and with a mare like Belle at my side, as long as she stays well, there really is no limit to the things that I can do and soon the whole of London will know my name.

13

Mounting the brow of a hill we come to a sudden opening, affording us with an uninterrupted prospect of the Thames. The trap door quickly flies open and my fare shouts at me to stop. My breath catches as the lights of all of the buildings and houses clustered along its banks reflect off the water like a vision of ancient temples. The man climbs out of the cab to further drink in the pure wonder of the scene and for a precious moment the silence is truly golden and the universe is at one.

'Look at it all!' he cries, his hand that of a general sweeping left and right. 'Factories, foundries, mills, inns, shops, all night apothecaries. I doubt that Babylon herself was bigger! And supposed to account for it all, here am I: bailie, lackey, busybody, taxman, bean counter, interferer-in-chief – sent to prod and poke and push things into order, and just my humble pen and ledger to keep things right. It is like asking to contain a plague of locusts in a butterfly net! All may laugh at me but without it, how could this place survive – where might it lead us and who would we be? The highways do not mend themselves. The lamplighters or street sweepers will not labour without pay. The common man, of course, thinks nothing of this and I am scorned like a pariah wherever I go!'

He looks to me for neither reply nor encouragement so I note the time and keep my counsel.

'This nation was ever founded on three things: its water, its commerce and its faith. All three are subject to the Law. At this very moment, I tell you, a large studio on Cheyne Walk is being emptied – boats arrive and leave with who knows what? Agents haggle over artefacts like holy relics, and the occupier, I am told, departs shortly for France. The churches and the cathedrals are deserted: the citizenry today worship at the picture galleries and the great exhibitions. They have seen the light and who can blame them? Art is big business – and that makes it my business. I intend, therefore, to pay them a visit to see that all duty owed is paid before the crown jewels disappear.'

'That is our destination, then?' I confirm.

He turns round as if in suddenly in remembrance. 'Yes, Mr

Carter – to Cheyne Walk. This sovereign is yours if you have me there in less than twenty minutes!'

It is indeed a princely offer but I have no intention of pushing Belle so hard, treading a fine line between setting a respectable pace and picking the safest path. My scheme is aided by the fact that our journey is made up on the hoof, a blend of horsey instinct and cab drivers' nous. The soft ground clearly suits her and she takes each dip and hummock in her stride and as we drop down to the river I burst with pride, rarely having seen the grey in such fine fettle. In just shy of half-an-hour we are there, crossing Albert Bridge and taking a sharp left onto the Walk, finding the area to be a hive of activity. Heavily-laden carts block the street, men struggle to make themselves heard and a rare commotion ensues outside one of the doors. As my fare disembarks he checks his pocket watch and lightly chortles.

'Tut tut! I am afraid I am unable to offer you the prize. I think we must have taken the scenic route. A deal is a deal, after all.'

'No matter sir.'

'I am grateful to you, nonetheless. It was a lucky chance I caught you. It appears that we have got here just in time.'

'Thank you, sir.'

'Your horse, Mr Carter…'

'Sir?' I wince.

'…is a magnificent animal.'

I touch my cap and breathe my thanks – but as he pays up and turns to go my curiosity gets the better of me and I cannot help but ask.

'The artist – who is he sir?'

The man swivels round in surprise.

'He is a foreigner, I believe. A type of a certain class. His name I do not know…but they call him The Man of the River.'

He turns again and plunges straight into the breach, yelling at the top of his voice and beating a path to the front door with his cane. At the same moment two men appear at a side entrance to the house that I take to be the tradesman's door, and, checking that the coast is clear, emerge with a very large object draped in a hessian cloth. They struggle to carry it down a steep grassy slope leading to the riverbank where I can just make out the form of a skiff; yet more men follow in procession, holding onto what looks like an enormous screen covered in a blue and gold daub. A tense conversation occurs before a light is extinguished and the nefarious craft rows into the darkness backed by a powerful tide.

Suddenly a great cheer goes up as the figure of a man - who I quickly recognise as my fare - is rudely ejected from the property by two liveried footmen, before getting back to his feet, roaring like a lion and brandishing his cane like a cudgel to force his way back inside – to an even bigger cheer from the crowd.

I decide that it is high time for me to leave and am about to do so when an outrageous Yank accent pierces the night air.

'Ha-ha! Would you look at that! Quite the thing we need, well, what, eh?'

I stare down from my seat: as queer a pair as you can imagine scuttle over to the cab. An elder man dressed all in white leads the way, hissing to his assistant who follows at his tails bent double under a stack of gilt picture frames, all the while checking furtively behind him. Reaching the step of the hansom and ignoring the rumpus at the porch, the chief turns a pale, monocled face in my direction and twirls his black moustache.

'Hold her hard now, driver!' he orders, motioning to the lad to lift in his load, both trying to fit into the cab. It is quite a riddle but they manage in the end and, once settled, I wait no further for instructions, clicking twice to Belle – then rattling east along the Embankment.

As I drive, I brood much over the words of the bailie and his savage verdict on the state of the Christian faith. Could what he said possibly be true? Keeping the river close to our right, every street corner that we pass on the north bank is home to a chapel, a church, a convent or a college. A stranger in town could easily be deceived into thinking this the most pious place on Earth – yet are these venerable buildings mere symbols only, built on shifting Thames sand and largely forsaken inside? Have our people really turned their backs on God and who will aid them, if not He, in their hour of direst need? I shudder at the idea and swear to redouble my pains as a true soldier of the Cross in the quest for London's soul.

Below me in the cab a quarrel is taking place, punctuated by a most alarming ripping sound. I have every mind to stop and call for the police until the hatch is flung open and the cause is plainly told. The young assistant's head suddenly appears, followed by his shoulders and an arm that propels an invisible object high into the air and far into the water. A splash is heard, followed by another, before he vanishes again and the argument resumes, bits of it in earshot above the hansom's clatter…

'Next! Yes – that one. Heap of junk that it is!' – 'But sir, the Academy!' – 'Academy what?' – 'The portrait!' – 'You mean this ugly dame?' – 'Yes!' – 'Next!' – 'No!' – 'Yes! Toss it out, toss it out! It ain't paid for anyway!'– 'But sir, your sketches!'– 'Do as I say!' –'

This precipitates an even fiercer debate and a loud howl issues from the cab, seconds later another head poking out – this time that of the chief. He shakes his mane of curls in the flow of the onrushing air and starts to stab and slash at a picture with a knife. Soon, this one too finds a watery grave and two, three, four ruined works follow until he heaves a satisfied sigh, disposing of the blade in a similar manner and calmly adjusting his necktie before diving back down. Unsure what to make of it all but noting that Belle is still quite calm, I steer us on into the city, the whole episode serving to remind me of my father.

For Joseph Carter, the great river was akin to a god – or rather, a goddess; riding by one of the many likenesses of Old Father Thames, I once heard him say: 'It is true that like a father she provides and she protects; but like a mother she also nurtures, nourishes, carries, teaches, beguiles…and eventually consumes.'

In his time as a nightsoilman he had once seen two creatures jump into its dark flow hand in hand, telling how the watermen who had witnessed countless more did declare that she was London's biggest morgue: 'First they throw in their things – then they throw themselves.' Ever it was, then, our New Year's Day ritual, like so many Londoners before, to walk to the nearest bridge and to toss in some precious object in tribute to the boundless munificence of the Mother – and to ask for another good year. For as long as Man has lived here she has held sway over our fate and been the gateway to another world. To cross her is always an emotion, an action that can never be vouchsafed, an affront against nature and a snub to her sacred realm. Yet the same sickle moon that hangs low over her tonight has risen ten thousand times before – and will rise again.

My reverie is interrupted by a sharp rap on the roof: 'This will do.'

In the cab there is more talk, more muted now, before the elder man steps out and brusquely strides away.

'The boy will pay,' he barks, without a backward glance.

Having reached Westminster I assume that their conveyance is done but the master fails to budge from his seat as he quietly surveys the turf. 'To the Alhambra,' he eventually declares.

'Sir?'

He has been snarled at ever since we set out and now his time has come to snarl at me in turn. 'Did you hear me not, you impudent fool? How dare you question me! Get me there at once - and at double-quick speed! - or else I shall report your number.'

His cut-glass English brogue grates on my ear as much as the erstwhile American's twang but in no position to argue and not game for a scene, I meekly obey his command.

'No sooner said than done sir.'

It is a short ride to Leicester Square but a tricky one: this is the twilit hour when the whole of London comes alive. At Wapping, foreign ships discharge their human cargo into port like swarms of flies hatching in unison from a corpse; in Shoreditch and Shadwell, workers pour out of the tanneries and head straight into the music halls; and here in the very midst of town, the streets are thronged with dozens of cabs and carriages all in a desperate race and with not a minute to pause. Folk fall over themselves in their frenzy, opportunity abounds and the newspaper sellers brace themselves as shopkeepers draw their blinds and bolt their doors. The sound of song and bawdy laughter spreads like the croup, and, for those who can pay, entertainment of all kinds can readily be procured.

After a few frantic minutes we draw up to the steps of the famous palace of varieties, lately of such dubious repute. It has only been a few months since its doors were last closed and its liquor licence temporarily revoked when the diversions on offer were found to stoop to other forms. If anything, though, the scandal has simply piqued the interest of the general populace and as long a queue as I've ever seen has formed around its perimeter, as a new wave of pedlars tout their wares and cancan dancers and men of substance mingle at the stage door. To such a place has the young gentleman asked me to bring him – but as he leaps onto the cobblestones his white-hot rage has relented and he is the epitome of graceful charm.

'You have done well, my man. How busy it is! Please keep the change and forget all that you have seen and heard.'

'Yes sir.'

'That volume that you carry,' he inquires, pointing to the bulge in my pocket as he retrieves a small easel from the seat. 'What is it? The Book of Common Prayer?'

He raises his eyebrows when I show him what it is.

'Revelations? There will be more of those before this night is out,' he titters, whistler of a merry tune as he melts into the crowd.

A flurry of fares leads us back and forth through the capital as we hop between the big hotels and the finest establishments, criss-crossing most of theatre-land. This is when a good mare earns her corn and Belle works with a sullen fury, deftly dodging a speeding growler and dancing through the eye of a needle so that at times I sit back and wonder what the reins are for. But all roads, as they say, lead to Mecca, and even my plucky grey will need a break, so when we drop off a patron at the Opera House I take the chance and head to the nearby Cabman's Rest.

Sited in the heart of Convent Garden, the square is abuzz with people, and I am glad to hand her over to the first boy who spots me, offering to double his usual penny if he treats her well. I take off my hat, wipe my palms and turn the handle to the shelter door.

Billows of steam pour from the hut briefly beating me back, forcing me to screw up my eyes and blindly step inside. Hit by a wall of pipe smoke and the smell of fried meat, I squint until I spy a free seat in the corner; at my entry all conversation stops and although I get one or two nods, the majority - including old comrades - avoid my eye as if fearful that by association my much talked about madness (when they'd say I'd gone 'east of Aldgate') might somehow rub off. No longer hurt by their reaction, I order soup and wait for the discussion to resume. Picking up a paper, I stretch out my legs and slowly start to relax.

The *East London Advertiser* leads with a report by the Temperance Movement cautioning the poor of the perils of ignorance and sloth, and there is more on the Trafalgar Square riots, the Police Commissioner accusing the protestors of purposely provoking his men. The copy also publishes a list of special events for the upcoming weekend, and, of course, there is the latest on the horrible murder of just a week ago. The article that really catches my eye, though, is about a travelling freak show of the 'strangest living curiosities' including a bearded woman and a man 'more beast than human, loathsome of visage'. I laugh out loud at the notion of such an apparition and decide I might go and have a peek, in the process receiving some dirty looks from the assembly, many cab drivers still unable to read and considering it uppity amongst one of their brethren.

The tension is eased when Annie, the straight-talking widow who runs the shelter, squeezes through and presents me with my soup.

'Ere you are, love. Don't mind them. Oh! – and we've got pease pudding if you fancies some?'

Nodding eagerly and tucking in, I turn eavesdropper to the men's honest banter…

'An Unfortunate, she was: a fallen woman' – 'They always call 'em that!' – 'Too right they do! But what I want to know is, 'fallen' from *where*?' – 'Not Heaven, anyway' – 'Hahaha!' – 'If you ask me, she was asking for it' – 'Course she was!' – 'Carrying on at that time of night' – 'Like we do! – 'We've all seen 'em!...'

It seems that they are discussing the hottest topic of the week.

'…Didn't *you* know her, Stan?' – 'I wouldn't say 'knew her'' –

'Prove it in a court of law!' – 'It might come to that!' – 'Don't tell his missus! – 'That'd be more than my life's worth' – 'More than hers, anyway' – 'Hey you! Don't speak ill of the dead' – 'Why not?' – 'Cos they can't speak back' – 'Is that a promise?' – 'It'd be the first time if it ever 'appened…'

And so on, and so forth.

In the end, I'm glad to finish my food and get ready to leave. As I do so, the hut door opens and a street helper enters, bashfully leading in by the elbow some half-starved thing.

'This 'ere squire wants a chop, darling. Can you cook one for him? He says he ain't had a morsel for three days.'

'You're not Salvation Army are you?' the man hisses suspiciously.

'Be off with you!' returns one of the cabbies. 'Stay 'ere any longer and it'd be better for you if we were!'

'This ain't a public charity you know!' puts in another.

The pair turn to go, when Annie speaks.

'Mr Ryan! Just you wait here and give me five minutes. I will cook *both* of you one with pleasure.'

The beggar's hunted expression clears in a heartbeat, his scowl turning into a smile as his saviour slaps his back in glee and escorts him to the nearest seat. Our hostess cooks and waits on the men without apology, serving up two steaming portions and standing hands on hips as the down-and-out devours his meal, bolting every mouthful and wiping his plate clean, eventually leaning back in his chair to collective ripples of disgust. To the amazement of all he then picks up my discarded newspaper and casually leafs through the first few pages, passing comment or giving his opinion on the articles that take his fancy…

'Dear oh dear. Bad business that! – Whatever happened to the land of free speech? – Half-a-crown? Daylight robbery! – Inquiry my foot! A whitewash more like! Take it from me, lads, heads won't roll…'

By now the irritation of the cabbies has reached boiling point and one old timer in particular has heard enough.

'Listen 'ere, mister,' he glares, 'You're quite the know-it-all, ain't you? Waltzing in with your hard luck story, preying on Annie's soft heart. But seeing as you're full to the gills now, here's something for you: if you know so much and we don't, what do you have to say about this?' He snatches up the crumpled paper and jabs a thick finger at likely the only word he knows - 'MURDER' - before resuming his seat to a chorus of approval.

'Well said, George!' someone cries.

'Not a moment before time!'

'It was probably him what did it!' cracks another.

At this, the hut falls quiet and the men glance nervously between themselves, in turn directing their gaze at the vagrant.

'No. Not me sir,' he replies softly. 'But I know the man who did,' beckoning to his accuser to hear him out.

The joker is not so cocksure now, getting to his feet under duress and edging over to the man's chair. Trembling, he bends down to the cupped hand.

'Hey? Who?' Lord almighty! Harry, Zachariah, come listen to this!'

The others join him, all agog.

'Cor blimey!' exhales one.

'The nerve...' retorts his pal, wiping his lips.

'I give you my word as an ex-guardsman...' the storyteller protests, suddenly sensing imminent danger.

Another of the cabbies is reaching up for one of Annie's saucepans. 'Bleedin' liberty taker. I'll teach you all about heads rolling – or so help me God!'

'You'd better scarper fella or you're going to hell in a handcart!'

'It's the gospel truth, I swear it! No, please!'

There is a loud crash, rapid footsteps and the bang of the hut door – then a stunned silence promptly broken by the peal of helpless laughter.

'You two make such a lovely couple.'

The boy looks up at me and beams. 'I really like your horse sir. What's her name?'

'Her name is Belle.'

'Belle,' he repeats to himself, '...Belle...'

'I can see that she likes you too. Do you have a horse of your own?'

'No sir. I'd like to though one day. I'd like to be like you.'

'Oh? And what about your father – what does he do?'

His face clouds. 'He is a skipper on the Thames.'

'Then why not you too?'

'He says that the river is dying sir and that his profession will soon come to an end. He says...' he hesitates.

'Yes?'

'He says that the hansoms have stolen all his work and that God has sent plague to the water.'

'I see.'

'The fishes are sick sir. He told me what that means. It's written in the Holy Book.'

I stare at him for a moment – then dig the volume out of my pocket.

'I do believe you're right,' I say, hurriedly flicking through the pages until I find it, a passage marked in red. 'Yes, here it is...well I never... "*A third of the sea was turned into blood, a third of the living things in the sea died, and a third of the ships were destroyed...*"

"*A third of the water turned bitter*", recites the boy, "*and many people died from drinking the water...*"

'Do you believe in that?' I ask him softly.

'Course I do!'

'Good lad. Here then is a shilling for your troubles. Keep it safe now and take good care.'

'Thank you, sir!'

An acrid sea mist swirls into the square, prompting me to pull up my cravat to cover my nose and mouth – and there she is, and just for a moment I see her: Alice, standing in her spot at the corner of the fruit market, in her pretty shawl and jolly bonnet and surrounded by her pails of yellow flowers.

Belle is spooked by a four-wheeler clattering by and once I settle her down and look again, the illusion has dissolved. Some of the haar must have caught in my throat for my eyes burn and the world seems full of mocking faces.

'You look like you've just seen a ghost,' the boy tells me.

'Not a ghost,' I reply, 'an angel,' wishing that Belle, like Pegasus, had wings too, so I might cut her loose and the two of us fly away from here to a simpler and better time: the time when love first bloomed.

3

Time Was (or Ten Years Earlier)

The day of the great annual Flower Show is here!

I have been up since before dawn feeding and dressing all of the horses, shovelling the yard and scrubbing the flagstones so that I can have a precious day off, and now I wait impatiently at the side of the road for my cousin Nell who has ridden through the night from Southfleet and who often travels the twenty miles or so to market to sell cherries and other produce from her family's farm. She is two years older than me and when she arrives I lap up all of her exotic talk, in awe of her news about the wider world and the ease with which she handles her giant black stallion, Comet, who answers to her every command. Today, though, is all about the fun of the fair, and I have a surprise in store too as we head to my own house on Albert Street to eat a hearty breakfast of kedgeree which mother is busy preparing.

Nell is confused when I ask her to secure Comet to the gate as I fetch a pail of water, then I lead her down the passageway to our small back-yard, making her cover her eyes and promise not to peep as I lift the latch to our makeshift stable. Nothing stirs and for a moment I fear the worst – but then a slight rustle and a snort comes from inside the shed and as if by magic standing right before us is the bonniest filly you have ever seen. Nell squeals in sheer delight and rushes over to the startled beast, throwing her arms round her mottled neck and planting her with kisses, and I marvel at the sight of this independent farmer's daughter behaving like a cooing schoolgirl.

'What's she called?' she pants.

'She don't have a name yet. We only got her yesterday.'

'You poor sweet cherub!' she exclaims, lovingly stroking her back and tickling her nose with a piece of straw.

26

'Guess what? Father's given me permission to take her with us today.'

'No!'

I nod excitedly. 'He says the sooner she gets used to the city, the better.'

'Oi! You pair!' a voice interrupts. 'Your food's going stone cold in 'ere and the table's set in the parlour – or don't tell me, you'd both prefer to eat outside.'

'Yes please!'

'Ooh, say that we can Aunt Jean!'

She pops her head around the kitchen door and her face breaks into a broad grin. 'You do surprise me. What are you like? Oh, go on then, seeing as it's you...'

We giggle like infants, hardly noticing the special meal which she has laboured over as we admire the vibrant tint of the filly's silvery mane and run our fingers through her shimmering tail. Much to my embarrassment mother decides to join us and as she fusses over the appearance of her only niece it is all that I can do to drag Nell away. The show, I remind her, won't wait for us forever, and with a new horse in tow I want to be sure to find a safe spot to watch from. In the end, she relents and even helps to fit the headgear as I respect my father's grave insistence that I see the filly takes the bit and we use some decent blinkers.

Slipping her out into the alleyway as she takes the place of Comet who will spend the day in the yard resting, we lead her in the direction of the public road, accompanied by a barrage of last-minute instructions.

'Now mind what he said: no messing about and don't let any-body feed her. Keep away from the main ring and for gawd's sake bring her back in one piece – or it's *him* you'll have to answer to, not me...oh, and cousin Eleanor: you're in charge. Do you hear me?...'

Eventually my mother's voice fades into the background, drowned out by the steady stream of vehicles already heading north. Half of Bermondsey seems to have had the same idea as we join a long procession of exhibitors, suppliers and droves of running children which only swells the closer we get to the river and I keenly feel the responsibility father has given me, more than happy as we walk for Nell to take the rope as she seems to put the filly at her ease. Passing by patches of scrub and new building plots that were once the fields of Horsleydown, we soon spy London Bridge, using the time to share our knowledge of the day's events and imagining how we might spend our little money…

'The first show starts at ten o'clock sharp,' Nell reminds me. 'Then it's the Punch and Judy.'

'Yeah! I can't wait to see Hackney Harris again.'

'Me neither! He's got a whole load of new tricks they say – and a dancing monkey.'

'What about your fella from last year?'

'Who?'

'The Little Russian.'

'Oh yeah! He was proper funny him.'

'Had you helping up on stage, didn't he? Took quite a shine to you!'

'Don't!'

'Ha-ha! It's the nosh I'm looking forward to the most. I'll eat jellied eels till I burst…'

'Ugh. You'll be sick – and I'll be in the dog house.'

'I don't care!'

'And I say I do!'

'And I say…whoa! Watch out!'

As we approach the bridge the road narrows and the scene becomes chaotic. Tempers flare and hackles rise as loaded carts vie with pedestrians and rival vendors, insults traded as folk bid to reach the crossing first. A huge pair of drays stomp through pulling a gaily-painted wagon fully laden with kegs of beer and the crowd parts like the Red Sea to avoid getting trampled in the crush. Nell and I exchange worried looks and I can see that the filly appears to tremble so we hold back, waiting for a slight lull before we take our chance to cross, managing in the end to hustle her over to the other side into the safety of Cannon Street.

Pausing for a break before going on to St Paul's, there is the usual bottleneck at Ludgate Hill and we are at a complete standstill for a full ten minutes, but as we find our way onto the Strand a carnival atmosphere prevails and the march has turned into a parade, lines of bunting festooned across the road, musicians striking up tunes and dozens of people leaning out of windows shouting greetings and waving merrily at the pageant below. As Nell passes me the rope again I also notice that the young horse is the subject of a few admiring glances so I push out my chest and tighten my grip a little as it occurs to me for the first time that she is a valuable prize and would make a ripe target for undeserving hands.

It is gone half-past nine when we find ourselves in Covent Garden and as we queue to enter the grand piazza it is no ordinary spectacle that we behold: costermongers caught in the rush are frantically setting-up stall whilst rows of women sit shelling walnuts, as fishwives selling cockles and whelks mingle with the hordes; a flower girl peddles 'Primroses, two bundles a penny! Sweet violets, penny a bunch!', as a grocer hollers 'Strawberries, all ripe, all ripe!' and stallholders aggressively petition passers-by 'What is it you lack? What do you procure?' A grizzled character of shocking bad hat tows his barrel organ to a likely-looking pitch just as a red-faced porter flops down onto a pile of sacks to take refuge under the morning edition. A tomato wholesaler registers his line of customers who jostle to buy from his limited stock, knots of boys play games of skittles and a packed omnibus spills over with passengers who scream and guffaw as they burst out of its doors. High above the square tightrope walkers and acrobats begin their acts and a strongman glories in seeing off a pack of roughs who try to push their way to the front of the maul.

The raucous din and wild kaleidoscope of colour are overwhelming even to a man – so I could easily forgive an animal who has only known the air of the chalk downs to be daunted in the face of such a hullabaloo. For our filly, though, nothing could be further from the truth as her nostrils quiver with pleasure and her muscles spasm so that only now do I start to understand: she shakes not in fear but in recognition, the scent of the freshly-cut blooms stirring memories of her Kentish home, prompting Nell to deem her 'a natural' for the hansom, exclaiming 'See how she loves it all! A little diamond you got there, Jez!'

Once admitted all of our promises are thus carelessly broken as we revel in the hustle and bustle, so far forgetting ourselves that we get drawn right into the thick of the action as we soak up the festive mood. Trick cyclists bob and weave their way around us, as fire-eaters play to the baying troops by singeing the eyebrows of the cowering front row; men in sandwich boards advertise the latest waxwork sensation, a shadow play draws gasps from a packed tent and mouth-watering fare of every possible kind is sold in mind-boggling profusion. Even as we bake in the soaring heat a troupe of performers is led protesting from the square for neglecting to pay their tolls, and, having bought pie and mash, we decide to fork out a precious tuppence apiece to go and see Madame Lee, the renowned fortune teller.

After a short wait outside a dwarf decked in bells solemnly pulls back the velvet curtain and the sightless clairvoyant signals to us to join her at her table. Nell goes first and I feel the hairs on the back of my neck stiffen as she takes my cousin's head in her hands and runs her gnarled fingers over every bump and indentation. Holding on, she rocks back in her chair and rolls her eyes, her throat producing a guttural moan like the rumble of water plunging down a ravine – until she abruptly gags, then speaks.

'I see…a white house and a garden full of roses. The wheat stands tall in the field and the goldfinch sings. You will have a long life and a goodly one.'

'Are there children?'

'Many. More than I can count.'

'Boys or girls?'

'Ah! That is your second question, my lovely. You will need to cross my palm again…'

Nell murmurs her thanks and as I shuffle forward the mystic sits bolt upright.

'Come closer child. I shan't bite! Now then, what do we have here?'

She reaches out instinctively with a skeletal arm to feel the filly's moist breath on her aged skin. Her hand hovers at the nose and then with the lightest of touches she starts to explore its head, her fingertips traveling up the unblemished muzzle, straying as far as the skull. The horse obliges by lowering her neck, seeming to accept - even enjoy - the crone's attentions, snuffling then licking the bony wrist that pulls me to her with startling strength.

'She is the salt of the earth, I cannot fault. Already she attaches herself to you in spirit – next will be in soul, a bond that can only deepen over time. She will be your guide and protector, the power at your arm, keeping a daily vigil at your side. Treat her badly and you will have lost a great ally – treat her well and her service to you will know no bounds.'

I listen rapt, and stare at the grey in new wonder.

'Yes,' she continues, 'quite a duo you will make. I dub you the Two Witnesses! There is no path you will not tread, no mountain you will not climb. For you, though, child, the road is not to be a straight one.'

My heart skips a beat. 'Madame,' I blurt out, 'what is foretold?'

'I see a life of plenty – up to a point.'

'And then?'

She purses her lips. 'Then I see a wall. Beyond the wall I see nothing.'

Behind me there is a sharp intake of breath and I turn to see that folk have been prying and the next in line are peering through the drapes.

'You see nothing?' one of them ribs. 'Course you don't: you're blind, ain't you!'

There is a riot of laughter and a scuffle ensues as the dwarf and another move to tackle the heckler. The fracas spills inside and the table is tipped over as Nell grabs the horse and tries in vain to drag me away, but stung by the prophecy I resist and cry out 'Am I not to have children too?' – to find that the chair is empty and the woman has gone.

Blinking our way out into the sunlight we make a beeline for an archway and discover that it is gone one o'clock and time for the main event. After the psychic's words Nell is still on a high and she blows some kisses to a gang of barrow boys who are busy rolling up their shirt-sleeves in preparation for the famous cart race. She then purrs at a line of chestnut geldings who parade by in their feathered plumes – yet as the cavalcade of brightly decorated floats rolls past, my eyes alight upon a vision of perfection, the most beautiful thing I have ever seen: a flower queen, barely fourteen, sitting in a rickety haywain, her long blonde tresses crowned with a tiara of pinks as she waves shyly at the crowd. In the midst of it all I try to catch her eye and she looks down at me and smiles and my head swoons, and I think my heart might just burst as the wagon slowly rumbles out of sight.

My cousin flirts shamelessly with all the farmhands, a marching band of pearly kings enters the square and we are serenaded throughout by an Italian harpist so that an hour passes more like a dream, but in truth much as those next to me are engrossed in the gala, my mind is somewhere else. Even Nell notices and asks me 'Is everything alright, Jez? You ain't half gone quiet,' and I stand rooted to the spot in a lovesick daze, a boy now half-a-man, hardly hearing or acknowledging her questions.

Once the madness of the race is over and the spectators have dispersed the drinking games begin and the show takes on a more sinister air. A comedian on stage is mercilessly pelted with rotten veg, a squad of peelers move in from nowhere to break up an ugly brawl and the grizzled old organ grinder has his hat swiped from his head and trodden into the gutter as local youths run amok. Giving the trouble a wide berth we end up at the corner of the flower market, happy to enjoy the displays of daisies and dahlias, China asters, cockscomb, lilies and bleeding hearts. I then drift over to one of the biggest stalls and as the girl cutting a ribbon for a fresh bouquet turns round, I find myself face to face with *her*: the mythical flower queen. She blushes and looks away and I in turn redden – and now Nell sees the whole story.

'I know her,' she whispers. 'Let me introduce you…'

'No!' I protest but it is too late and before I know it she is behind the stand.

'Alright girl? Don't you look a picture! You never met my cousin Jeremiah, did you? Jez, this is my good friend Alice.'

A weak 'Hello' is just about all I can muster.

'Hello there,' she replies politely. 'Nice to meet you. I hope Nell's showing you a good time…and who's that hiding behind you?'

'Oh,' I croak, 'this…is my horse.'

'I can see that,' she snickers, coming round to the front of the stall. 'You're a proper beauty and no mistake! You're quite the belle of the ball.'

'That's it!' cries Nell, 'Belle it is!' and the name is destined to stick.

Alice looks puzzled, then declares 'Wait, I've got something for you…' returning from the stall a few seconds later with a garland of marigolds which she throws over the filly's head. 'There you go, petal,' she chirps, 'now it's you who's the flower queen!' and I feel like I'm floating on air.

Nell winks at me craftily and excuses herself to get some sugared nuts, leaving us with the newly-christened Belle who is soon the centre of attention as children flock to meet her. The horse, though, looks distracted and Alice asks her, 'Here now, what are you after? You're not thirsty are you, my love?' pricking my conscience as I realise I haven't watered her for hours. 'Not to worry,' she soothes, pulling a bunch of daffodils from a pail and watching her as she takes a long cooling draught. 'That's nice I'll bet. Drink as much as you like. You'll soon be right as rain.'

Belle empties the bucket and snorts with satisfaction when out of the blue Alice asks 'Hey, can I sit on her back?'

'Erm…' I hesitate, not really liking the idea but feeling that it would be rude to say no.

'Oh please!' she implores with her big blue eyes. 'What harm can it do?'

'Alright,' I cave in, 'I don't see why not.'

To her credit Belle is as good as gold as Alice struggles to climb on top of her and get into position; her ears prick up, though, as a rowdy rabble barges past us, Nell is hurrying back shouting at us and frantically waving her arms, and then right behind me someone lets off a firecracker and in the blink of an eye the filly rips the rope from my hand, throws her blinkers and is off like a shot. 'Belle!' I cry but she has bolted and all I can do is run as Alice clings onto the grey's mane as she cuts a swathe through the crowds, baskets of wares sent flying and folk diving for cover as she leaves a trail of pandemonium in her wake.

Showing me a clean pair of hoofs, I lose sight of her in the chaos and my cousin yells at me to cut her off at the main exit to the arcade before she can reach the busy highway on Garrick Street. Making the portico first, I follow her traces through the roars of angry vendors and the odd blur flashing past the gaps in the stalls, gawping helplessly as a stack of bales sets alight and Belle rounds the bend chased by a mob of bystanders, poor Alice holding on for dear life as the horse hits the cobbles and charges straight towards me. Just then, a porter with boxes balanced on his head starts to cross the gangway before freezing as he sees the mount bearing down, the filly swerving at the last moment before skidding to a halt as I jump in front of her and scream 'Whoa!', propelling Alice out of the saddle as she somersaults through the air and pitches into a cart-load of sunflowers.

Time stops. Nell goes pale. Then, from a sea of yellow, two eyes tentatively peer, as pure and blue as the sky above as she starts to giggle, then laugh, then roll around in stitches, and as folk rush over to help her I close my eyes, take a new breath and give silent thanks for the mercy of God – and for the miracle of Alice.

The journey home seems never-ending as we decide against retracing our steps so as to avoid another mauling at London Bridge, crossing instead at Waterloo and making a big sweep round via the Elephant and Castle.

My cousin is full of the joys, nattering ten to the dozen and regaling me with every detail of her furtive tryst with a childhood sweetheart...'So he says...and so I says...', and the sun has long set when, having returned to Bermondsey with leaden feet, Nell collects Comet and we agree to meet up again as usual a few days in advance of hopping time.

Belle pulls hard on the rope towards the smell of hay and I am no match for her raw power, all fingers and thumbs as I remove her bridle, fill the manger and hurl in a few forkfuls of dry straw to top up her simple bed. The back door is locked so I return to watch in weary contentment as she munches away, in the end deciding to join her as she takes a last drink and lies on her side. I blow out the candle, snuggle in and curl my arm around her, my brain whirring with a hundred new sensations and a tender face etched forever across my heart, before my head drops and I quickly fall into a deep and dreamless sleep.

*

More than a year has passed since that balmy day spent gallivanting north of the river.

Things are different now and so am I: older, wiser perhaps and entrusted with broader duties, I also harbour grand ambitions of my own. Much to the surprise of my father, after speaking to the owner of the yard I have decided to apply for a cab licence of my own, tired of being at the beck and call of every man jack so that in a matter of weeks I will get an official number and it can be another's chore to do the mucking out. Not a day has gone by when I have not thought of my beautiful flower queen and every morning before work I kneel in the nave of St Mary Magdalen's and pray I will see her again. Yet as the months drag on everyday life blunts even the sharpest lines of recollection so I am no longer sure our star-crossed meeting was not a cruel and twisted fable.

Even the priest has noticed that I have become a more fanatical church-goer, signalling his approval with a paternal pat on the head as he walks by – until one day my faith cracks and I ask him.

'Father Cronin?'

'Yes? What is it, Master Carter?'

'Father…when we ask God for something, does He always give it?'

'That depends on what you ask for,' he frowns. 'What is it that you want?'

I squirm and stare at the floor.

'Ah, I see. An affair of the heart. Well, young man, we've a saying where I come from: *What's meant for you won't go past you.* That said, my advice is this: trust in Jesus and torment yourself no more with foolish notions of love. The Lord works in mysterious ways and even I can't pretend to know what He has in store. Forget about this girl, whoever she is.'

'Yes, Father.'

But even as I said it I knew that 'forgetting' Alice was the one thing I could not do.

The leaves are falling from the trees and the long nights drawing in before I am finally freed from the confines of the yard. I am chaperoned and shown the ropes for a mere two days until I am deemed fit to go it alone – then the play-acting stops and the real business begins and the prospect of the open road is mine.

Belle has turned four years old and is considered a mare now, so it is only natural that I pick her to pull my cab. She is ready for the work and her sinews ache for labour and after a month on the job she glides like a thoroughbred. I, for my part, make my mistakes early on, treated to a few harsh lessons on the politics of the hansom by customers and other drivers alike, and as the routine of the day gets under my skin my private agony over Alice slowly wanes, lessened by the knowledge that as of yet I still have nothing in the world to offer her and thus no real means to win her hand.

Delighted otherwise with how things are turning out, time heals me in a way I could never have predicted but I still maintain my morning ritual in the empty pews, praying instead for the improved health of my ailing parents even as I take unabashed pride in my new role as the family's main breadwinner. Exhausted at the end of each full day and completely wrapped up in my job of maintaining and operating the vehicle, as well as in learning the ever-changing cost charts lest I am unlucky enough to be hailed by Madame Caroline Prodgers or some other self-appointed guardian of the Law hopeful of tripping up and ruining an otherwise honest man, I finally abandon all thoughts of courtship and romance, my hopes for the future invested squarely in the shape of the hansom – and the many talents of Belle.

It is a pleasant change, then, when one evening cousin Nell drops in on us on her way home from market. She seems well but fidgety and has a mischievous glint in her eye and after enjoying what hospitality mother can provide she presents her with a bumper bag of crop, asking that I come with her to help fix an issue with the cart which she has left outside the pawnbrokers, next door but one. No sooner have we left the house, though, than she grabs me and presses something into my hand.

'What's this?' I ask, staring at the mud-stained envelope.

'A note,' she beams, her cheeks shining.

'A note? From who?'

'From a well-wisher who wishes you well…'

'Me?' I blanch. 'What does it say?'

'How do I know, silly! Why don't you just read it?'

I feel an overwhelming urge to flee to some dark and secret place so that I can stall learning the note's contents for as long as I desire; instead, put on the spot and under hefty pressure from Nell, I reluctantly tear it open. It reads: "SUNDAY. 2 PM."

The Mass is the longest and dullest I can ever remember and father, who still insists on attending church, is plainly vexed at my half-hearted response to the liturgy. No offence is meant but he limps homeward in a black mood, incited into speech only when I tell him that after lunch I plan to take Belle out for 'an afternoon gander'.

'Just as you wish,' is his curt response.

'Am I to take it that you do not approve?' I ask him.

'The Lord's day is a day of rest,' he bristles. 'Does the mare not deserve time off as well?'

'Yes, of course father…but I thought –'

'You thought you'd make up your own rules. Oh well, I'm sure that you know best.'

'I only wish to go a little way.'

'Hm. I suppose next up you'll be telling me you're opening your own cab office.'

I stop in my tracks, hurt by his accusing tone.

'I had hoped,' I answer carefully, studiously avoiding his gaze, 'that my choice of profession pleased you.'

There is a heavy pause and now it is he who stands like a statue, head bowed in self-reproach. 'Forgive me, son,' he rasps, 'and take pity on a stupid man. I am old and tired and ready for my grave.'

'Father!' I scold him. 'It is not like you. You have many good years ahead of you still!'

'I think not, though it cheers me to hear you say so. No: you are the master now and know your horse better than I.' He looks up. 'Ah, see! Here is your mother. Do not speak of this – it is time to eat and be merry and - if my nose does not lie - beef and onions awaits us at table.'

Overshadowed, however, by his uncharacteristic outburst, lunch is taken mostly in silence. Wary of the time, I prod at the glistening meat, skip desert and make my excuses, nipping into the yard at the first opportunity to ready Belle for our pending rendez-vous.

'Will you be gone long?' father asks, having kept on my heels.

'As I said, it's just a gander round.'

'With a saddle and panniers on – and you in your Sunday best?

'Father...'

'Fret not, son. I have been there myself once – your mother and I weren't joined in the womb. Here's a crown - yes, keep it - what use is it to me? Perhaps you can treat her to something.'

'Treat who?'

'A girl likes to be made a fuss of,' he persists, 'and you must appear quite the catch: every inch a Carter of Bermondsey. How could she not be impressed?'

'Thank you, father,' I defer.

'It is not me you need to thank,' he says, as I start to trot away. 'Fare ye well, go easy on the mare...and don't be home too late, Jeremiah...'

I stand in the drizzle under the piazza clock. It is eerie to see the square so deserted and as the minutes pass I am filled with the con-viction that it has all been a misunderstanding. I start to wonder why Alice would want to contact me such a long time after our only meeting, doubting that she would think well of me given the events surrounding our introduction.

Having started on the cabs it would have been a normal thing for my work to bring me past this part of Convent Garden on an almost daily basis; as I earned my spurs and grew in confidence, however, I made efforts to steer well clear of the area to avoid re-opening a healing wound and when the demands of a fare made such manoeuvres impossible, I had not yet chanced upon her at that sacred corner of sweetest memory. Added to that - and knowing the way of the world - it simply could not be that such a comely lass was without her share of hopeful suitors. Yes: the whole thing was an elaborate practical joke and I had been reeled in like a Dover sole – hook, line and sinker.

Yet as the clock chimes the quarter-hour the honest joy of Nell's countenance on giving me the note pops into my head and I decide to wait for a minute more. Then, out of nothing, Belle's ears prick up and I hear the distant clip clop of another horse rapidly approaching.

'Come on, Bracken – giddyup!' I hear a girl's voice urging, and I turn around to see not a horse but a pony cantering into the square – a garron, or maybe a Welsh cob. The mount is also burdened by the weight of a second rider, a young fellow about my age who I soon recognise as an apprentice from the Isle of Dogs forge.

'Hullo – what are you doing here?' he greets me in surprise.

'I might well ask you the same!'

'My sister Alice…' he begins, before the same realization dawns on us, and we regard each other in numb shock.

'You two know each other!' the girl shrieks, her face partly hidden by her hood. 'I told you he was a nice boy!'

'Yes…' he grimaces, allowing her a fleeting smile.

'My brother had insisted on joining us today - dotes on his baby sister, don't you Will? - but now there's no real need for him to come along, is there?'

He swithers for a second, then sighs, 'I suppose this does put a whole new slant on things…' and Alice claps her hands in glee.

'You must promise to be back by six o'clock though,' he implores. 'I'll find myself in Queer Street if you don't...'

'I promise!' she laughs, dismounting and reaching up to hug him. 'Here. Six o'clock. I give you my word.'

With her brother gone we take a walk out together, finding ourselves truly alone for the very first time. Hardly knowing each other our conversation is stiff and unnatural as we talk about the weather or point at other couples huddled under umbrellas yet still determined to enjoy a leisurely stroll. The company of Belle, then, is a timely and welcome distraction and the perfect foil for all those awkward pauses as she does her best to cause mischief, making Alice scream by nibbling at her cloak and lifting her tail at the most inconvenient moment so that it is only as we arrive at the walls of Hyde Park that we begin to relax and speak more freely.

'It was a great surprise to get your note,' I tell her. 'Nell even brought it to my door.'

'Dearest Nell – oh my!' she gushes, 'I nearly didn't send it – changed my mind three times – it was her what persuaded me – hardly got a wink of sleep – worried I was making a dreadful mistake!'

'No!' I cry, with a bit too much passion. 'I mean, no...not at all.'

'I'm so glad – and by the way, I'm sorry for being late today. Old Bracken was playing up something rotten and I got myself into an awful muddle. Father was acting strange as well: I'm sure that he suspects us.'

'Mine too,' I chuckle, 'though I suppose this kind of thing is much easier for boys than girls.'

'Is that so?' she asks, before adding, 'and what kind of thing *is* this exactly?'

'Er...well...I'm sure I didn't mean...'

'Only kidding!' she teases, quickly letting me off the hook.

'Tell me then,' I ask, itching to hear the whole story. 'What made you decide to write?'

'Saw you one day, didn't I – or, rather *her*,' indicating Belle. 'There isn't another like her in the whole of London town! Then, I noticed you - driving the hansom you were - and I says to myself: *Now there's a fine figure of a man!* Thought nothing of it though till one day I mentioned it to Nell and she reminded me that I'd met you before, and, well, you could say it got me thinking…'

'So I have Belle to thank for all this?'

"Belle?' she pats the horse. 'Is that what they call you?'

'Actually,' I tell her, 'it was you who gave her her name.'

'Me? I don't remember that. You're just being silly now – although I have to admit it don't half suit her. Gosh, how could I ever forget you! Quite a merry dance you led me on – nearly got me killed!'

'Oh dear…you apologise – don't you Belle?'

The mare tosses her head and Alice tuts. 'Apology accepted Belle! It wasn't your fault you got a fright. Be good today and we'll say no more of it.'

As if on cue the skies lighten and I exclaim 'What a sun there is! It seems a pity to waste it. Here, give me your cloak and I can keep it in the basket.'

But at this she checks her stride and her carefree demeanour vanishes. 'I have something I must tell you,' she warns me.

'Yes. What is it?' I ask her, my heart suddenly gripped by an icy sense of foreboding.

In answer, she simply raises her hands and pulls back her hood. The left side of her face is graced by the first pink flush of womanhood like a new rose coming into bloom and I realize how much she has changed, if possible even lovelier now than first time I saw her…but as she turns to face me I struggle to stifle a cry of anguish as I see that the other cheek has been marred into horrible discord, pitted, pock-marked and badly blemished by the work of some disfiguring malady.

'Now you know,' she nods, her expression resolute again as I strive to steady my emotions. 'I fell ill not long after the fair,' she confesses, 'and soon took to my bed. The local physician was sent for and by the time he arrived my whole body was on fire and I was mad with pain and beside myself with fear. His visit was a short one for he held out no hope and gave the tidings I was dreading: I had succumbed to the pox.'

I cannot help but groan so she stops briefly to compose herself before bravely going on.

'The next few days are a blur for I was in the throes of a fever and dreamt I was speaking with the dead. My family took it in turns to nurse me, never heeding the danger to themselves – and after a week I was told I might live. The scars will be with me for life and I have only the sight left in one eye. Still, I know I am one of the lucky ones and that I should be grateful for everything I've got.'

'I'm sorry,' I murmur. 'I never knew…'

'Why would you?' she blurts, before her tone instantly softens. 'It was three months until I next saw Nell and by then, although I had lost a few more battles, I had finally won the war and wished never to hear its name again.'

For a time her story renders me silent but eventually I offer some token words.

'You have suffered terribly – that is clear to see; unlike some, though, you have survived. All things happen for a reason and this is surely God's sign that you are part of a bigger plan.'

'You think so?' she laughs bitterly. 'Life is certainly different now and I take it day by day. I no longer get the compliments I once used to and people I knew keep out of my way – but sometimes I wonder if it is more a blessing than a curse.'

I think of bluffing by saying nothing has changed; Alice, though, I can tell, sees through it all.

'Look!' I cry instead, as a four-in-hand speeds by. 'Let us go and find a place in the park. I have brought us a picnic and we can sit in the sun and watch the fashionable folk ride by.'

'Oh…very well,' she agrees, even raising a smile as we take our turn to enter through the celebrated archway.

In the afternoon light the South Carriage Drive looks its picturesque best and together we choose a spot under an ancient oak as I tie Belle to the railings and roll out a wool blanket. The ground is carpeted with hundreds of red and gold leaves and as the sound of a brass band playing 'Rule Britannia' drifts across the Serpentine I pour us some lemonade and dish up some jam and cake, snatching a glimpse of Alice's slender frame as she watches the ladies taking the air in their magnificent landaus. The sheer gaiety of the scene seems to bring her out of herself and we sit there for what feels like hours with not a reason to move, she sharing her knowledge of flowers and trees, I remarking on each passing equipage, Belle browsing peacefully on the lush sward a few yards behind us.

'Ow! What's that?' Alice jumps, and I swiftly crawl over, gently removing the ladybird from her puckered cheek as it opens its wings and flies away. Our eyes meet and something passes between us as she puts a finger to her lips and gently caresses my hair. Later, on one of the secluded pathways, she quietly slips her hand into mine and I feel ten feet tall as I lead her back to Covent Garden seated on the back of Belle.

It is still not yet six as we near the square but at the sight of her brother waiting her giddy mood changes and her feelings close up like a clam.

'We must do this again,' I brightly suggest.

'I have had a lovely time,' she admits, 'but perhaps we ought not to.'

'But...why ever not?' I recoil, cut to the quick by her reluctance.

'You're sweet,' she sniffles, 'and I like being with you...but I think it would be for the best.'

'I don't understand.'

'Oh, Jeremiah!' she rebukes me in exasperation, before descending with my help and re-adjusting her hood to once again conceal her face. 'No man would want a woman who looks like this – least still a wife.'

'I do,' I tell her, yet she shakes her head sadly and without another word starts to walk across the piazza.

'No: Alice! I mean it...' I call out, but her brother moves to greet her and the two quickly fall into deep collusion, my love out of reach and the moment already gone before I have the pluck or wit to sway her further.

*

The snow falls continually and all the streets and pavements are coated with a dirty brown sludge, and as I blow on my fingers and rub my hands together we join the fast-moving queue at the cab

43

stand. The rank is mobbed by hordes of patrons trying to escape the bitter winds and I know it will only get busier as the day progresses and that the weary Christmas shopper will pay nearly anything to be picked up and taken to the place they call home.

It is the shortest day of the year and as such should be my shortest shift, for my licence permits me only to work the hours between dawn and dusk – but experience has taught me that it might be one of the longest and that the bad omens of this bleak December morning are merely the start of a day of relentless graft; a prospect that is made all the less appealing by the small disagreement that took place between Alice and I as I got dressed and prepared to leave the house…

'Jeremiah?'

'Yes, my dear?'

'Won't you stay with me today?'

'You know I want to – but I must go and fetch Belle.'

'I feel sick again.'

'Here: take a sip of water.'

'No…I couldn't. I do worry about you out there you know.'

'It's only for a few hours, my dear – then I'll be back.'

'If you really wanted to you could put in for a day off at the Yard.'

'Really Alice! Another few days like I have had of late and that new house is as good as ours.'

'I don't care about that and what is the money to us? We have everything we want.'

'Nearly everything. It is not just about the money anyhow.'

'Oh? What then?'

'I have responsibilities - duties - I can't just come and go as I please.'

'Sometimes I think you love that hansom more than you love me.'

'Don't be ridiculous.'

'I'm not.'

'Come on now – this isn't getting us anywhere and I'll be late if I'm not careful. Look: I promise once this winter's over you'll have things more your own way. I'll even drop a shift if you want me to. You know I miss you – don't you?

'Hm.'

'And that I'm doing all this for us?'

'I suppose so.'

'Good. Well give me a kiss goodbye then. That's better!'

'Be careful Jeremiah!'

'I will.'

'Don't push yourself too hard – and please take this rug with you! You'll catch your death in the frost...'

I kill the cold by withdrawing into a world of wholesome memory, playing the game and going through the motions so that from the time I collect my first fare the images turn over in my mind's eye like a treasured album of faded daguerreotypes: Alice running like a child through a shallow stream, her bare feet splashing water everywhere and soaking her thrifty summer dress – Alice again, opening an envelope and shedding tears of joy as rose petals scatter to the floor – Nell bouncing uncontrollably at the news in a dusty barn – my father in a top hat as he drives an open carriage up to the church gate after coming out of retirement for one last hurrah.

The vintage picture show is interrupted only by the need to deal with practicalities such as the halters freezing and the wheel fixtures getting clogged with ice and salt. Alice's plea - *'Won't you stay with me today?'* - still rings in my ears as I push on and vow to make it an early finish, my love for her burning more fiercely than ever, a delirium for which no quack has yet concocted any viable cure. Clocking off, however, is not so easily done as a series of arctic blasts whip up a churning maelstrom in Mayfair, prompting stranded people to stand in the middle of the roadway as they try to commandeer any passing vehicle only to find seasonal good cheer in short supply.

Though my official cut-off time is past it would be more than my life is worth to attempt to ignore or abandon those in need; indeed, there is a well-understood clause in the small print of our permits which obliges any cab driver to carry on working if to do so is clearly in the public interest. That being so, I grit my teeth and turn into the raging blizzard, chilled to the marrow and hardly conscious of who I carry or where I am going as a deathly white coverall is thrown over the stricken city.

In the chaos items of random rubbish and empty boxes are sent flying into our path, one smashing into the legs of poor Belle who has been slipping and sliding all over the cobbles making me scream blue murder, petrified that the hansom will upturn. In the end, I call a halt in a sheltered side street, invoking a further clause that a cab may cease to operate if either injury or illness to horse or driver renders it impractical or unsafe to continue. Just as I am considering whether or not to send for the veterinary, another hansom pulls up beside me and I see to my surprise that it is the deputy from the Yard.

'Jeremiah! Where have you been?'

'Samuel! Egad! It would be easier to tell you where I haven't.'

'I've been looking for you for hours – we have received an urgent message that you must return home at once.'

'Why? What is wrong?'

'There has been some kind of accident: Alice –'

I wait no more. Cracking the whip, I yell at Belle to run like the wind.

Hampered in my efforts by the river, I know that it will take no less than half an hour to travel to my door but I lean forward in my seat as if by willing it so I can somehow get there quicker. It is a vain hope, though, as the mare struggles to keep her footing, the cab veering wildly from left to right as a slab of snow comes crashing down from a shop roof engulfing a miserable chestnut seller. I ride on with total disregard for the conditions, immune to Belle's cries of pain and guided only by the gaslight – many lamps out as others flicker sporadically like lone beacons in a storm at sea.

Losing the feeling in my fingers, I am already weighing a new future and listing the things I want to say to my wife: how life is going to be different now and that I have finally learned my lesson; how she is all that really matters to me and that I should never have left her today; how I am a fool who does not deserve her and will do anything to repay her trust. I will gently remind her of the days not so long ago when we had to fight for our love – days when the whole world seemed against us and everyone questioned her big move south of the river to chase a hopeless dream. I will talk about the blissful months of our early engagement, our mutual affection having reached its most delicate stages and her scars and self-doubt only making me want her all the more...but more than all of this, I will tell her how it is still my most cherished wish for us to start a family together and to have a child of our own, and that, notwithstanding our setbacks and our bitter disappointment, we should put our fortunes in the hands of Fate and give it another try.

Eagerly holding onto such ideas, I arrive back in Albert Street.

The shop sign above the pawnbrokers is swinging manically in the wind squeaking a ghastly air as window frames rattle and shutters bang against the bricks. Reaching the house, all is in order but there is a strange light from within that bathes the front room in an eerie amber glow. I abandon the cab and open the door.

Hurrying inside, I hear the sound of low voices in the parlour and as I head through I can scarce comprehend what I find as two figures stand next to the table stooping over Alice's prostrate form. Hearing my step, one looks up at me - the night-watchman with his Bull's eye lantern - and sombrely shakes his head, whilst the other - a doctor, I presume - walks up to me and puts a supporting hand on my arm.

'Mr Carter? I have been waiting for you. It was a neighbour who raised the alarm. It looks like she tried to come downstairs for something and must've tripped halfway. I left my post and came as soon as I was notified but when I got here it was already too late. I'm very sorry: I'm afraid there was nothing I could do.'

*

In keeping with her wishes she is buried next to her mother, making one last journey across the Thames. After the funeral, I do not visit for a very long time.

I know now that I will never love again and that Christmastide will be forever be tainted – a time of taking that can only ever mean one thing: the time when Alice left me, taking away all my dreams and the last hopes of the Carters with her.

Time was when we walked together, scheming our schemes and dreaming of a better life. Time was when she would tarry at her stall at the end of the day in the hope of seeing me pass by…and time was when she would leave a candle at the window to welcome me home in the grey hours of the gloaming.

But that was another life, another world, another way. That time has passed and the light has gone out and the dream of love is out of time.

Time was. Time is. Time forever will be.

4

Spring-Heeled Jack

How long I have been riding in circles for I do not know, but untroubled night, so they say, gives counsel best. Not that there is any hope of that here as we roll up outside the Lyceum just in time. Filtering into the rank, the doors of the theatre fly open, emptying a huge and hysterical crowd onto the Strand.

It is the show that has gripped the whole of London: *Dr. Jekyll and Mr. Hyde*. The American actor, Richard Mansfield, in the twin lead roles, has cast a spell over and terrified audiences for the past month, some to their wits' end, so that the play has been the talk of the town throughout August, a boon for men such as myself who toil to generate significant trade on the hot summer nights. For nearly five weeks now it has been easy pickings as every hansom congregates here at around half past eleven, sometimes even managing a return trip to snaffle any stragglers, all high as kites and unusually happy to part with their precious dough. In fact, I have heard so much about it from my various fares that I have a fancy to go and see it for myself – if ever I could get a night off, that is.

Basking in the reassuring warmth of the vestibule lights, parties rave over the genius of what they have just seen, but tonight - as with every other night since the early days of the production's run - there is an added edge to the excitement in the air as ladies in particular look around nervously in the unspoken knowledge that we have a killer in our midst. Lingering outside longer than usual, the mild air no doubt still pleasant in comparison to the sweltering heat of the stalls, all heads turn as a loud cry of 'Oh! Murder!' is heard, instinctively taken up by two or three more. The effect is like setting a light to touch paper: panic ensues, people start to run and a volley of warnings boom from one street corner to the next. In the melee the orderly line at the rank goes all to pot leading to a heated shoving match, and a respectable enough looking couple don't miss a trick and slip past the ruckus to nip in front.

'Do us a favour, fella and take us to a cheap hotel,' the man implores me.

'In you get!' I shout, and no second invitation is needed.

He helps her up and as I try to get clear of the chaos it becomes apparent that all is not quite as it seems as a blood-spattered maiden is chased around by an axe-wielding fiend hollering, 'Another woman has been murdered they say!' and I realize that this is the doing of a rival theatre company whose comic version of the same play is on offer just a few blocks away. Whilst there are one or two groans from those in the know, their misguided publicity stunt has badly backfired, some girls sobbing and irate husbands swearing like troopers as the players are set-upon by the seething masses and forced to beg for their lives.

It is time to exit stage left and drive north to Soho.

I drop them off at the only establishment that will care to take them at this hour: a seedy little lodgings just off Old Compton Street. The place is half dilapidated hostel, half glorified bawdy house with an ever-revolving door. As the subdued pair are shown inside a narrow passageway another couple rudely push their way out and hail me for a ride. The heavily-muffled man slurs an unfamiliar address 'near the marches' so I ask to see his money first, prompting him to chuck a handful of coins at my feet and order me to 'hold your horses' as his companion for the night straightens her hair and flattens her grimy petticoat.

I had occasion to frequent this area in the not-so-distant past and so became acquainted with the existence of these clandestine businesses, for a time becoming a well-known face in the immediate purlieu. It is surely a wretched life for those who work in such places, though they are a rung above the nightwalkers and the common Unfortunates who pour in their needy hundreds onto our darkened forecourts – yet theirs is still a despised and dangerous living…more so than ever, of late.

London after midnight is no place for a woman, as recent shocking events have shown. A faceless evil stalks the city streets and the blackest of moods has descended upon its people the likes of which I have never known. Three of our womenfolk - fallen women, but our own fallen nonetheless - have been cut down on our watch, making us look twice at all men and second-guess the meaning behind every innocent action. Some say it is Spring-Heeled Jack returned for another reign of terror over his hated and cowering subjects; others say that it is the Devil himself or a mortal emissary sent to do his bidding; more still call him the 'Knife'. But the ugliest rumour is that it is a cab driver who is responsible – for how else could a man get away with cold-blooded murder in the middle of the greatest city on earth and then vanish into thin air? Folk lock their doors at night, the police are at a loss and the East End is a powder keg ready to explode. Men roam in packs, the worse for drink and ripe for vengeance, so that I hasten to work not out of tardiness but in fear for my life.

For a place so accustomed to gore and violence there is yet something new and disturbing about these murders. Who is he, this demon, lurking in the recesses and waiting to pounce like some dread sentinel of the gaslight? What wrongs does he seek to right, what slights must he avenge? And if in the height of summer he is bold enough to act as public executioner what outrages dare he stoop to in the cover of winter's depths?

Some say that his prey are heathens who care not a tuppence for their lives and would be led like Passover lambs to the slaughter – yet in my pity for them I wonder if these women are not the true saints or martyrs of our times. Tempted, trampled upon, tried and torn asunder, they are the mirror of the blessed Christ as he stood before the Sanhedrin. But nay! The idea is monstrous - blasphemous even - and I must not allow myself to admit such weakness for if we are to advance our civilization and truly raise a 'second Troy' then those who sin should find no shelter and all the rotten apples must be cleared from the orchard.

Disease or cure, one thing - and one thing alone - is certain: for as long as this Angel of Death is abroad he has his iron shackles fastened tight over Albion and:

'Black the cloth in heavy wreaths folds over every Nation.'

Heading ever norward, we pass beyond the reach of the last of the oil lights and the ken of the horse patrols: the Tottenham Court Road, Hampstead Road, then Camden High Street, onto a lonely stretch leading up to the Heath that some have dubbed the 'murder mile'. The olden haunt of highwaymen and lowlifes, cutpurses turned cut-throats, the area is a no-go at night and generally avoided and is said to be plagued by the spirits of the dead restlessly searching for their stolen things. I, however, never refuse a fare, pressing the book in my pocket if ever I feel fear, knowing that it is not the dark or silence that really kills us.

I slow down at a bend in the road at Red Lion Hill and somewhere nearby a church bell rings. At the request of numerous clients I have left the trap-door open to allow a pleasing through-draft into the cab and I cannot help but catch a few snippets of the relations taking place below me…

'Shove over and take your paws off me, will ya? You promised you'd show me a good time tonight.'

'And so I will! I know how to treat a young lady with style.'

'I'm expecting more than this!'

'Just wait until we get there. Then you'll see.'

'You'll say whatever happens to be in your head. I don't believe a word of it.'

'And you'll say anything – but your prayers.'

He bellows at his own brilliance and she kicks out and struggles as he leers, 'Just behave now and gis us a kiss!' My blood boils so I give two clicks to Belle to make her pick up speed as we take the steep incline to the wide-open spaces, hoping that the cooler air will chill his affections, coming in sight of the baleful Gibbet Tree.

There are places of death dotted all over London and this solitary elm has been the end of the line for many a wrong 'un, strung up and kept dangling there until their bodies cooked and crackled in the sun. As we pass I almost expect to feel the spectral hand of a cool brigand come to rest upon my shoulder but the only phantom around here is my drunken benefactor and at the sound of another screech my patience finally snaps so I pull hard on the reins and the wheels grind to a halt.

'Sir?' I call out.

No answer.

'Sir!' I repeat with gusto.

'What is it man?' a voice barks back.

'Your journey is over.'

A ruffled head peers around the trap and stares out into the darkness. 'Another furlong or two more should do it, driver.'

'I said I go no further.'

'Oh did you?' he retorts. 'Ach, very well! This is good enough, I suppose.'

He vacates his seat with no little fuss, roughly seizing the woman by the arm as she swithers in following him onto the scrub.

'Hold up! Where are you taking me to now?' she asks him.

'All in good time,' he snarls, starting to lead her away down a footpath towards the distant lights of a known gypsy encampment.

'No!' she resists. 'I won't come if you won't tell me.'

'Is that so?' he stares at her madly. 'Well, we'll soon see about that...'

She yells in protest as he grabs her by the hair and berates her 'Do as you're told you cheap little trollop or I'll knock seven bells out of you!'

'You'll do no such thing.'

The man stops in his astonishment and two piggy eyes regard me with a mixture of loathing and contempt.

'You?' he jeers, before blithely resuming his assault.

'Let her go,' I insist, running by him to block his only way.

He halts again, mutters a vile oath and lowers his head like a sow about to charge, but I hold my ground and as he sizes up his target he has second thoughts, divining something in my stance and stare.

'You've got a neck,' he drawls. 'Who the hell are you, anyway? A jumped-up errand boy – that's all.'

'I'll show you who I am.'

I take off my hat, uncurl my whip and lift my cape, my shadow enveloping him as I face him anew in the moonlight's all-revealing silver.

'But…what infamy is this?' he draws back. 'No, it cannot be…'

'Down, snake!' I command him. 'Onto your knees! Now it's you who'll learn to say his prayers.'

His knees buckle and he crumples to the floor at the sight, as I brandish the Book and he begs for his salvation.

'Repeat after me…'

'Spare the life of a miserable sinner!'

'I saw Heaven's gate open and there was a white horse…'

'I'll give you money, gold, whatever you ask for!'

'Repeat!' I chastise him, as he feels the lick of the lash…

'Its rider is called Faithful and True - repeat! - *His eyes were like flames of fire and many crowns he wore upon his head. He had a name written on him but no one knows what it is. His robe -* louder! - *was covered with blood. His name -* say it! - *is 'The Word of God!'*

The snivelling wreck crawls in the soil, clinging to my boots.

'Tell me your name.'

'My name,' he gasps, '…is Wilkes…'

'Mr Wilkes: you will pledge to take care of this woman and if needed see her safely home. You will never again use one of God's children. Defy me at your peril for she is under my protection and if I learn that any harm has come to her or those who need her, I vow I will hunt for you like a dog and verily smite you down.'

'Yes! I swear it. I will see that it is so!'

I address her in turn. 'If you desire it, miss, I will convey you back to town.'

'Thank you, sir,' she shudders, 'but I am happy to take my chances.'

'Winsome wench!'

'Not for you!' she turns on him. 'No, nor for me; only for them.'

'Then get out of my sight.'

Scrambling to his feet, the man lurches towards a grove of trees like flushed quarry, and, lifting her petticoat, she scampers in his wake.

'Be careful, now!' I warn her, and she looks back at me and nods before being drawn like pollen in the breeze into the beckoning beyond.

*

The desolate heath is beautiful at night-time, gilded a brilliant yellow by a swathe of gorse in full flower. I step up onto the plate, scraping my hair forward before replacing my hat and sucking in the sweet, unsullied air.

I sing softly to Belle as she munches on some sedges, her tail flicking to keep the nocturnal insects at bay. Feeling a sudden thirst, I unwrap a stick of liquorice and am about to call time on our brief respite when the mare starts and rears up in alarm. Detecting movement, I reach for my whip again – yet it is not a desperate footpad who emerges from the bushes but a bedraggled trio of waifs and strays. Clarted with mud, as thin as rakes and white as ghosts, the smallest of them having seemingly lost a shoe, the eldest scrutinises me with deep misgiving, holding back the restless youngsters who seem keen to break cover and interfere with the nervy grey.

'What are you doing mister?' one of them boldly pipes up.

'I am working,' I tell them, 'but never mind that. What's three leverets like you doing out and about at such a time of night?'

'We was having a rest, that's all.'

'A rest?' I smile. 'A likely story. No good, I'll gladly wager.'

'No sir!' the lad responds with real feeling. 'It's not that way at all. We are on our uppers and truth be told we all got scared. We meant no harm, I'm sure. Give us a minute more and we'll soon be on our way.'

My heart softens. 'I care not a jot what you do. I'm sorry if I sounded unkind. Where is it that you head?'

'To Lambeth,' he declares.

'Lambeth? That is some journey on foot. What business takes you there?'

'We are making for the Workhouse for the one here is full – it's that or I take the Queen's shilling. My employer has accused me of stealing and I have lost my situation. I could hardly leave my brother and sister behind me, so the three of us are going together. We've walked from Highgate already – is it much further?'

'Another five miles at least.'

Their faces drop at the news and the little one starts to weep. 'Oh, Annie!' he sobs. 'My feet are sore. I don't think I can stand it.'

'Nonsense, Thomas!' she rebukes him. 'Don't be such a baby! We need to be there by dawn or we're done for!'

I stare down at them as the girl digs out a hemp purse and empties the contents into her tiny hand: a farthing or two, at best. She gives a look of despair but the eldest just shrugs, the spit of myself at his age. I bite my lip for although I would not normally countenance such an arrangement, I cannot in all conscience leave them lost and alone on this perilous wasteland, and as it is my intention to return to the city forthwith, I ignore my misgivings and invite them to 'Hop on board.'

'Pardon me, sir,' the lad frowns, 'but I'm not sure what you mean.'

'I mean exactly this: get in, the lot of you, but hear me out straight. I'll brook no tomfoolery whilst you're in my cab or you'll find yourself at the roadside. Keep your voices down and when I tell you to, get under this here blanket. I'll take you as far as I can then you'll have to make your own way. Do me a favour now and darken those two lanterns – Belle here will keep us right.'

Encouraged by their big brother the other two climb in, bringing with them the remains of a dry half-loaf and a small bundle tied to a stick. The lad looks around, puts out the lights and jumps in beside them.

I head first north, then east, before bending south again, sticking to the rutted back roads; we pass a bleak farmhouse, a ruined barracks and the Soldiers' Daughters' Home. A thin rain starts to fall and having blacked-out the cab the lane is indistinguishable from the verge, the moment when a man is dependent on his mount if his destiny is not to be the ditch. I wonder how far I will dare to proceed in such a risky fashion as we skirt the stagnant water of an old moat house – just the sort of place where in living memory 'Jack' once sprang.

If I told the tale of the full exploits of this babbling and baffling ghoul - a prankster, a brute, a bear; a bogeyman, a fool - then you would surely believe that I spoke in jest of the antics of a pantomime villain; a creature, folklore has it, who prowled the hamlets and villages, grasping at servant girls with his clammy hands before jumping to his freedom over nine foot walls, laughing as he leapt. Yet I could hardly be more serious. Hear tell of a miscreant who dons a helmet and oilskins and revels in causing post-chaises to crash, and this will naturally stir emotions of repulsion and indignation; then take the same rogue, ascribe to him a few foul acts but this time give him a name and you have made a man into a god, turning common rumour into the stuff of paralysing myth.

Better, you might say, to turn a blind eye and let each new day unveil its worst. Ignore it and in doing so at least deprive the culprit of the satisfaction of acclaim…but in our own evil times it is not so easy to look away from the bodies being carted off the streets or the death notices of the defiled. Much as we might try, we cannot absolve ourselves of blame by seeking to pin these latest horrors onto some vague or diabolical foe; for the plain fact is that these crimes are the work of a human hand, and the bulk of Christendom has been roused against a Beast who in reality moves amongst our number. Would I know him if I saw him and what do I look for? A satyr breathing blue and white flame? One would expect the author of such brutal deeds to carry the mark of his sin in the lines of his face – but perhaps he has all the appearance of a respectable burgher, masked rather than given away by his all-too-familiar mien.

It is just as well that this latest threat to our city's fragile order currently goes without a title - a player without a part; a tyrant without a crown - and long may it remain, for I do not think that the much put-upon people are capable of taking much more, and a catchy new nemesis, however vulgar or contrived, might just tip them over the edge. He follows, of course, the bad histories of many a mountebank - The Great Garrotter, The London Monster, The Hammersmith Ghost - who at one time or another pitted man against the unknown and briefly held extraordinary influence over us all. Yet this one, I fear, is here to stay. How right was the Poet who said that a great part of the trouble that vexes the world arises from our words and how lucky it is that the gift of the golden voice belongs to more than just one man!

An owl hoots at our passing and from out of the hedgerow a dark shape suddenly emerges, springing across the track in front of the cab. I do my best to brake but there is a dull thud and a howl of pain, making the children scream in fright before the thing gets to its feet and pitifully limps away.

'Are you alright?' I call down to them.

'I think so,' the girl answers. 'What was it that just jumped out?'

'Oh, it was nothing,' I tell her, trying to sound as calm as I can. 'Just a wild animal – a large fox or something of the kind.' Yet I know very well that it was no such thing and that, whatever it was, it was no ordinary creature of copse, hill or field that I, or any rider, would know or recognise.

The closeness of it all makes my teeth start to chatter and yet the swift return of mirth to those below and the renewed drumbeat of Belle's hoofs soon combine to dispel any morbid thoughts. After all, I tell myself, over the years this lawless city has had more than its fair share of murder – if anything can be fair, or truly shared, about the killing of another. Yes: there are wicked places and the roll-call of the innocent dead is a black chronicle of our shame; but if we can only learn to live again like God's chosen people then the land of milk and honey is ours. Perhaps, too, when it comes to the endless fight against Evil there is much to be learned from the hardiness of the small ones and guileless beasts of burden, and we should put our faith in those who trust the most and seem to know the least. As for me, my epiphany will surely come and I will wait patiently for the world to take shape around me. My only task: to follow the road to the Time of Reckoning when a higher power shall sift my life and gather the harvest of my days.

*

In a few minutes I look up to see the Bishop's Palace on the horizon and in what seems like the blink of an eye we are back in the bosom of what is sometimes called civilization. I hiss at my illicit cargo to 'pipe down and cover up' for if I am found to be in transit at night with three unaccompanied minors then I will be hauled before the assizes faster than you can say 'Spring-Heeled Jack' and difficult questions are bound to be asked. For once, though, the high road is practically deserted and I am allowed to proceed unchallenged, relieved to have emerged back into the light and to be in sight of holy ground.

It was my intention, if possible, to go as far as the north bank but buoyed by our easy passage I have a better plan. Crossing at Horseferry (and crossing myself at the same time) I steer the hansom all the way up to the Palace's gatehouse, warning the children to stay in their seats and striding up to the portico only to be instantly surrounded by sentries in tunics bearing the Archbishop's coat-of-arms.

'Halt! Who goes there?' the Captain barks.

'A man of God and a Christian.'

'Turn about and hold up your arms!'

'Really sir…'

'Frisk him well, Tristan – then examine his coach.'

'No!'

'Eh? He argues! Well, well, well. What do we have here?'

One of the guards shines his light directly into the trap and gives a cry as three sets of eyes peer back at him.

'I can explain…'

'You better had,' he snarls, pointing the tip of his sword at my throat, 'or a long stretch in the cloisters awaits you.'

'They are orphans in need and I stumbled upon them by chance. Their plan is to enter the Workhouse but I thought that the Bishop might be so good as to take them in.'

'Oh! That was your idea, was it?'

'His Grace has retired for the night and will see no-one.'

'Perhaps, then, he might at least share a cup of kindness?'

'Kindness?' splutters the Captain. 'What kindness is shown to us who spend every winter stamping our feet with not so much as a thimbleful sent our way from the Bishop's cellar? His Excellency will rise for naught but the Holy Ghost – and only then if it has sent its calling card. If it is kindness you want, better go to the Seaman's Mission.' He looks again to the faces in the trap. 'Is this man's story true? You son! Answer me and do not lie!'

'It's the gospel truth sir – or may the Lord strike me down!'

'A modern Good Samaritan, eh? Was he armed?'

'Only with this, Captain.'

The guard throws him my book.

'Hm. Just as well!' he grunts, staring at it briefly and tossing it back to me. 'Let me suggest then, sir, that you stick to reading and leave salvation to others. Here, we cannot afford to turn the other cheek and, as you might recall, not much good came of the early preachers.'

I wince but do not reply, retaking my seat and carefully directing the vehicle to whence I came. Lucky to retain my liberty and a mite crestfallen, I need a moment to re-order my thoughts as I decide what to do about my three stowaways.

If the highest apostle in the land will not deign to give them shelter then at least I can do something to smooth their way. Cutting down Paradise Street, I turn right onto Lambeth Walk, in just a short trot bringing them to the main entrance of the gloomy building, outside of which a queue has already started to form. Telling the children to get out and summoning them to my side, I point to a tiny chapel opposite.

'Head straight over and you will find it open. If others are inside then take a seat in a quiet corner. At around four o'clock a verger will come and give you some broth. Ask him for shoes and if he says 'no' put this into his poor box for he often has a pair or two kept aside. Then, by all means try your luck at the Workhouse but be careful not to carry any change – for if the taskmaster finds so much as a groat on you then he will strike you off his list and rejoice in showing you the door.'

'Thank you, mister!' they sing as one.

'You are welcome,' I say, nearly urging them to put their trust in the church but then thinking the better of it.

I wish, too, that I could join in with their innocent joy as they scurry across the road to their next new adventure; but though I am no seer I do not share their hope and wave them off with a heavy heart and a strong inkling that on entering the institution they will merely be swapping one predicament for another.

Still, I have a job to do and creditors to pay and it is high time I earned my keep tonight. Cajoling Belle, we swing round and make for Bethlehem - not the starry little town but the lunatic asylum - serenaded on the way by the plaintive pre-dawn chorus of its various unlucky inmates, very much alert and attune to the orbits of this mixed-up world where the impoverished are punished for having money, the mad kept apart from the sane, and the keepers of the keys of sacred knowledge sound asleep in their feather beds.

5

Bloody Mary

To all the constables and cabbies she was known as 'Polly' but to me, for the year or so that I knew her, she was always Mary – or Mary Ann.

I had first seen her - or at least noticed her - one hot and muggy evening in June or July of the previous year, arguing with a flustered landlord and shamelessly causing a scene before being pulled to one side by a passing policeman who began by reading her the riot act and ended up watching with weary despair as she snatched up her belongings and stomped away. Such skirmishes were nothing out of the ordinary with Mary, at least towards the end of our brief acquaintance and especially so when she was back on the gin, her presence at any of a hundred street corners given away by her sharp laugh and well-oiled singing voice, so that she was often heard before she was seen, letting you know in advance the colour of her mind and what knockabout version of fickle old 'Polly' a mounted troubadour could expect to find. Yet despite dozens of such encounters from the summer of 1887 to the early autumn of 1888, three instances in particular stick in my mind from when our two paths were destined to cross, the smaller details of which were to come flooding back as I sat and gave evidence in a packed and stuffy courtroom on the second day of her inquest.

I'd spent the whole of the morning of September 3rd in the draughty waiting room of the Working Lads' Institute on White-chapel Road, waiting in vain for my name to be called as I sat, a virtual prisoner, kicking my heels and staring at brooding skies through grimy windows until eventually, at midday, the courtroom door opened and whosoever remained to listen were duly informed that the session had been adjourned for lunch and that we were now free to make our own arrangements as long as we returned by one. Fifteen minutes later, as I let my bowl of skink cool at a nearby oyster bar, I had plenty of time to remind myself that how I'd come to be there in the first place was nobody's fault but my own.

It being a Monday, the previous day had started out as a typical Sabbath as I took my three hours' rest before rising, washing and dressing and having a light breakfast, then making my way out into the street, and, upon satisfying myself that the weather was to stay dry, meandering in my own good time to my chosen Sunday service. Many a moon had there been since Father Cronin had stood waiting to welcome the weekly worshipers to St Mary Magdalen. With him, a big part of me had left Bermondsey too, and the fiery new faith I had found again through our reunion did not extend to stomaching the bland fare now on offer under the bloodless young rector tasked to fill his boots.

In contrast, at the open-air pulpit at Hyde Park Corner, I was met by no such scenes of quiet observance, only anger and a rising panic as word continued to spread of the latest outrage of three nights past. Even the lay preachers had taken heed of the newly-restless mood, abandoning their planned tirades and addresses on chastity to instead draw directly from more suitable teachings first taken from Job and then - I well noted - the Book of Jeremiah, with its message on how to react in times of fear and great peril:

'Return, all of you who have turned away from the Lord;
He will heal you and make you faithful!'

In the upset and confusion of that tense afternoon, fleeting images from Thursday's nightshift revisited me like dark angels so that later on when I at last had some peace and solitude as I made my way back to Albert Street, I began to wonder if I ought to make myself known and report all that I had seen and heard in another night from hell.

It had been anything but the day I had expected but I knew if I said nothing I would neither sleep nor settle. That being so, I paid

63

a visit to the police station on Paradise Street before emerging into the dusk a full two hours later, arriving home sore-headed to take my supper much later than I was wont.

Ready to retire to my room to get some much-needed rest before the start of another busy week, I heard a knock at the door and on opening it a messenger boy handed me a telegram, scampering off before I had the chance to glean its contents. Inside, to my great surprise, I found an order in lieu of official summons, instructing me to attend the inquest of Mary Ann Nichols, to be held the next day at the WLI and to commence at nine o'clock sharp.

*

I had no sooner retaken my place in the waiting room when the door opened and I heard my name called to be the next witness. Ushered into the brightly-lit wood-panelled chamber and directed to take the stand, the murmur of voices fell silent at the sound of my lone footsteps on the bare wooden floor, so that only as I turned to look at the public gallery did I realize that there was not a seat to be had, the front two rows seemingly occupied by members of the Press who peered at me intently, whispered to one another and exchanged hastily-scribbled notes.

Looking back towards the bench and the various officials, I felt my mouth go dry and my palms moisten as a pale-faced clerk solemnly swore me in and the bald, bespectacled coroner loudly cleared his throat before getting straight down to business, asking me to confirm my name, address and occupation.

'My name is Carter, sir - Jeremiah Carter - of 12 Albert Street, Bermondsey. I work as a hansom cab driver.'

'And your age please Mr Carter?'

'Twenty-eight sir.'

'Thank you,' he nodded, checking something, then picking up another piece of paper and reading as if from a script. 'Mr Carter…you have been called here today as a witness at the inquest of Mary Ann Nichols. In the course of proceedings you will be asked a number of questions and you must answer as best you can. If you do not understand a question then you must say so and if you do not know the answer then it is far better to be honest than to give a reply that might mislead this inquiry. Have I made myself perfectly clear?'

'Yes sir.'

'Good. For the record, then, can you confirm that you knew Mary Ann Nichols?'

'I did sir.'

'For how long did you know her?'

'I have known her - knew her, m'lord - for nearly a year.'

'Can you also confirm that this is a photograph of the deceased?'

He waited as a court official handed me a print.

Hit like a slap to the face by the black-and-white image, it took a moment for me to give my response. Then: 'Yes. That is her.'

'How did you first come to meet?'

'Well, Your Honour –'

'This is an inquest, Mr Carter, not a criminal trial and I am not a judge. A simple 'sir' *will* suffice.'

'Yes sir. I first saw Mary several months before I spoke to her, in what would have been midsummer of last year. But I never met her properly until the October time.'

'How do you know that it was in October?'

'Because of the circumstances in which we met. It was the time of all the trouble at Trafalgar Square. Like the other cabbies I was doing my best to avoid the place. One night, though, I dropped off a fare at the top of Curzon Street and decided to head back to the cab stand on Northumberland Avenue. It was a soaking wet night with a bitter east wind. The rain was freezing as it fell. As I rode by, she ran out from somewhere and flagged me down. 'Please help me!' she cried out. 'I've not a penny to my name but I have a ticket for a night in a lodging house. I will die if I have to sleep out in this cold and my blood will be on your hands!' 'Well, that's charming!' I thought – but I did feel sorry for her. She looked desperate, her ripped bustle was flapping in the wind and I could see that she was soaked to the skin. It is against the rules, I know, but I gave her a lift. The lodging house was only a ten-minute drive away. I trust that this will not be held against me?'

'I can assure you that it will not, Mr Carter.'

'Thank you, sir.'

'That, then, was the beginning of your...friendship with Miss Nichols?'

'Yes sir.'

'Pray be good enough to continue.'

'Well...after that our paths seemed to cross more often. Perhaps it was just that I noticed her more – or maybe she sought me out. Either way, she would give a greeting or a wave if she saw me, for I think that she remembered what I'd done for her. For my part, I suppose I developed something of a soft spot for her – that having helped her out once I now saw it as my duty to make sure she kept bad at bay. To be frank, our chance meetings caused me no real anguish; in many ways, I looked forward to our occasional chats and over time I got to know her better.'

'Indeed! And what, may I ask, were your exact relations with Miss Nichols?'

'My relations?'

'Yes. How often did you see her? How well do you suppose that you knew her?'

'It is difficult to say Your Honour – I mean sir. It depended on where our business took us. Some nights I'd see her on several occasions; at other times, I'd see neither hide nor hair of her for weeks. I'd say that we had no more than a casual acquaintance though I admit I was fonder of her than the others.'

'The others? Who do you mean by that?'

'Meaning the other women who'd usually be...out and about.'

'You knew of her profession, I take it?'

'Not really.'

'You did not guess?' he persisted.

'I suppose I had formed an opinion of it.'

The coroner rubbed his head and made a show of sifting through a small pile of documents, pulling out two or three.

'Mr Carter: I note that thus far you have referred to the deceased as 'Mary'. From statements provided already by others I had understood that she was generally known as 'Polly'.'

'She was.'

'But you differ. Why is this?'

'That's an easy one, sir. I remember not long after we'd started to talk, I'd asked her one day to tell me her name. 'Polly,' she snapped back at me, without an ounce of feeling, like the very word was hateful to her. 'Something's amiss,' I told myself so at our next meeting I took the bull by the horns asked her her real name. She glared at me for a second – and if looks could kill!...but then the storm clouds cleared and she smiled at me just like a little girl. 'My right name,' she told me, 'is Mary Ann but even my own relatives don't call me that! If you really like, though, you can call me Mary.' And, well, she let it roll from there.'

'She was conferring an honour on you perhaps?'

'Perhaps. I think that she trusted me and, besides, I believe I was the only one who'd ever taken any interest.'

'Did your 'interest' in Mary Nichols extend to more than friend-ship?'

'No sir!'

'And hers in you?'

'I very much doubt it. It wasn't like that between us.'

'It never is, Mr Carter, it never is…' he remarked, prompting the first outbreak of muffled laughter in court.

I was, I admit, somewhat thrown and unsettled by this early line of questioning, laden as it was with suggestion and innuendo as to the true nature of mine and Mary's bond, and devoid of all due sensitivity and sympathy for the feelings of her family and friends, who, I presumed, were somewhere in attendance. Still, I was a novice to such proceedings and had to accept that the coroner was simply doing his job and must not be seen to be weak or show favouritism, however difficult the case may be.

His opening salvo, though, I was soon to realize, was merely the warm-up act for the main performance of the staining of Mary's name, and, by association, of nearly ruining mine. Moving first to the question of where she originally came from and how she'd come to live in the East End, I told him truthfully that my knowledge of her past was patchy, limited to whatever she had chosen to tell me – and the bits she had let slip when too much liquor had loosened her tongue. In explaining this, I called to mind a much more recent encounter which I had had with her in the July just gone, recalling it vividly as the time when I'd found Mary at her most optimistic, carefree enough to joke about and have a bit of banter and with none of the many worries on her shoulders that were soon to lie in store...

'Tell me more, Mr Carter, of this happy occasion that you allude to.'

'It was just a few weeks ago, sir, for I remember it was St Swithun's Day. It had been a very hot day and try as I might I'd struggled to get any sleep. In the end I gave up, heading early to the stables and making the most of the extra time by joining my horse in her stall and rubbing lotion into her pelage, where the horseflies had taken their lunch. As the sun went down and it started to cool, we headed out onto the road –'

'I didn't ask for chapter and verse Mr Carter. Please get to the part concerning Miss Nichols.'

'Yes sir. I bumped into Mary just a few hours later. She was standing in a queue by the Aldgate pump. Seeing me, she gave me a shout. 'Well would you look at that!' she hollered. 'Where've you been stranger? I ain't seen you in a month of Sundays!' 'Deary me!' I answered. 'I thought I was dreaming there! I could say the very same about you!' Laughing, she left her pail and hurried over, and as she made a fuss of my mare I couldn't help but notice that she was looking rather good, clean and neatly-kept, with a bit of colour in her cheeks. 'You look well!' I told her. 'How have you been?' 'Not too bad, thanks!' she replied. 'Been away, ain't I? Living the good life and with a bed of my own.' 'Whereabouts?' I asked her. 'Out Wandsworth way,' she said. 'A different world to here.' 'Very nice if you can get it! How did that come about?' I asked. 'It's a long story,' she winked at me. 'How long have you got?' 'Not long at all,' I said, '– so get a bleedin move on will you!'

'Just as you like,' she smirked, with that funny wrinkle in her nose. 'I'd had a bad time of it, as you know, and had to enter the Workhouse so at least I got to spend Christmas indoors. It was horrible – and I ain't ever going back! Then, I got discharged to service to a most respectable couple. It was dandy for a while but in the end I got itchy feet, so…here I am.' 'What you doing now?' I asked. 'Oh, nothing much. Enjoying my freedom.' 'Well don't enjoy it too much!' I joshed. 'I won't. I got plans, anyway,' she confided. 'Off to see my children soon, though none of them know it yet.' 'I'm glad to hear it,' I told her. 'Make sure that you do. There's nothing in this world as important as family, Mary.' At this she nodded but scowled slightly, reminding me of how the topic of her children had gradually become taboo – a far cry from when we'd first got to know each other when it had been 'Henry this' and 'Eliza that'; yet as time went by she'd made reference to them less and less often, as if even the mention of them was too painful to her and the memory of their times together too hurtful for her to recall. Her attitude towards her ex-husband had also really hardened and she seemed to blame him for many of her troubles, which had started - in her eyes at least - the day he cut-off her allowance –'

'If only that were so, Mr Carter!' the coroner interrupted. 'Sadly, this inquest has already heard much evidence to the contrary. It seems that Miss Nichols was the cause of her own downfall, her insatiable taste for alcohol the font of all her woes. Indeed, Mr Nichols did all he could to help her – some might say, went way beyond what any man could reasonably be expected to do for such a troublesome and ungrateful wife. I personally believe that he was entirely warranted in his course of action and that his only mistake - if he made one at all - was to continue paying her her allowance for so long.'

'If I may say so, sir, I think that is a little harsh.'

'Do you now? What do you say then, Mr Carter, when I tell you what so many others have lined up here to tell me: that she was a wastrel, an adulteress, an unfit mother, whose own flesh and blood had practically disowned her? What would any right-minded man

69

in my position think, upon learning that here was someone who had once had everything a woman could possibly wish for: a loving husband, a stable home and a brood of children playing at her feet? She threw all of this away – and for what? A life of sin and wretched idleness and walking the streets alone at night to scrape together the money for her 'doss'. If that is not enough, it pains me to tell you that just a few days before the meeting you describe - July 15th, was it not? - Miss Nichols had left her position in service in disgrace, absconding from her employer having stolen his property to value of three pounds and ten shillings gross.'

I looked down, unable to find a ready answer to the many charges he had laid at Mary's door.

'Yes: it is a sad truth,' he concluded, 'and one to which we here in court are privy far too often, that a woman without a husband will never come to any good.'

I could not deny that the coroner's extraordinary statement explained much of what had happened and accounted both for Mary's prolonged absence and her unheralded return, as well as filling-in many of the blanks in her life that she herself had never sought to address: her fall from grace and the reasons for the break-up of her marriage; the close proximity of her mother and sisters in Knightsbridge yet her insistence that she live a life of hardship alone; and, most recently, the short-lived reversal in her fortunes and the sudden availability of hard cash which I had naively put down to the charity of a mystery benefactor or else an unknown piece of luck but that had, all along, been too good to be true.

In the harsh glare of the witness box and with what felt like the disapproving eyes of the whole room upon me, I felt as if the wind had been sucked right out of my sails. As I had arranged for a local carman to bring me to Whitechapel that morning, for once in the guise of passenger, I had had a little time to consider and prepare the things I wished to say, hoping in some small way to be able to act as Mary's advocate in a cruel world that had at first conspired to drag her down and then succeeded in dragging her under. Instead, it seemed that with every statement and recollection, I was only adding more grist to another page of the official report that would see her history sullied forever and her reputation, such as it was, destroyed beyond repair.

Hardly acknowledging the coroner as he declared his intention to 'move swiftly on' to the 'sad events' of the night of Thursday, August 30th, I found myself wishing I had never offered my assistance to the Law and so avoided altogether the painful ordeal I was now being forced to endure.

'Mr Carter…in your statement to the police which you made yesterday, you claim to have both seen and spoken to Mary Ann Nichols during the night in question – or rather, at 2 o'clock the following morning, that being Friday, August 31st. In other words, you met with her not two hours before her sudden and violent death. This means that, in all likelihood, you are one of the very last people to have seen the deceased alive. As such, I would like you to give a full and frank account of your encounter with Miss Nichols, including what you had been doing immediately before you saw each other as well as what you did after the two of you parted ways.'

'Yes sir,' I swallowed. 'I will do my very best. In the first part of the evening I would say it had been a fairly normal night. The main roads were busy and the pubs and inns were packed; the mood was good and I had not witnessed any trouble. At roughly 9 pm, though, in the space of a few minutes the streets emptied as a bright orange glow lit up the sky. Drawn to it, I ended up riding down to the river where an enormous crowd had gathered at the South and Spirit Quay to watch a warehouse all ablaze, with the gallons of water poured on it by the fire brigade making no difference at all. I sat and watched for a while myself - quite a sight it was! - but in the end we left them to it and returned to our work. It was pretty dead until the time when last orders was called – then, all of a sudden, the streets which had been so quiet swarmed with red and anxious faces, all looking to secure a cab or carriage to take them home out of the rain. From midnight up until two o'clock in the morning I never knew a slack moment. At such times an unscrupulous cabbie can practically name his price; that, however, is not my way, and I worked solidly to assist as many people as I could, regardless of whether their conduct merited it or not. I had just dropped off another patron on Old Montague Street when a woman appeared from out of the shadows and as I saw her sway and stagger I quickly realized that it was surely my friend. 'Mary? Mary Ann? Is that you?' I called out to her. 'Hey? Who's that?' she turned around. 'It's me: Jeremiah,' I said. 'What the hell are you doing?' Sizing me up with half-squint eyes, she pursed her lips then blurted out, 'I'm not doing nothing! Go away. Please leave me alone.' Pulling her brown ulster tighter around herself in an effort to keep dry, she made for Brick Lane and as I was now not engaged by anyone in particular and could see no new call for my services, I decided to follow her in the cab. Making an effort to keep a discrete distance between us, I watched her as she made very slow progress across the dirty roads and along the broken pavements, stopping every thirty yards or so to take a few deep breaths and sometimes propping herself up against a wall or holding onto a set of railings before rousing herself and somehow continuing on. Concerned for her welfare at such a lonely hour and, I admit, curious as to her intended goal, I kept on her trail as well as I could; yet with the burden of the hansom and the poor state of the roadway, I soon lost her in the jumble of narrow lanes and darkened passages where even policemen fear to tread.'

'Miss Nichols could not possibly have been lost then?' the coroner asked.

I shook my head. 'No sir. That place was like a second home to her. She knew every nook and cranny.'

'It's clear, though, from your description, that she was 'the worse for wear.''

'There's no denying she'd had a few drinks in her that night. Nothing unusual, I'm afraid, with Mary. How much it affected her, though, is another thing, for she had wit enough about her to double-back on me and sneak up behind the hansom, giving me the fright of my life when she reached up and shook my raised seat. 'Oi! You! What've you been following me for!' she roared at me. 'Hey missus! Don't you ever do that again!' I warned her, even as she cackled. 'I'll do just as I please if you won't leave me be!' she insisted. 'I'm sorry – but I was worried about you,' I told her. 'Isn't it time you went to bed?' 'Probably,' she frowned, 'but I ain't got one tonight. I've had my doss-money three times today and spent it all.' I asked her if a two-penny hangover wasn't good enough for her. Or even a penny sit-up. This finally got her laughing again – at least for a moment.'

'How do you suppose that she had come about her money three times?'

'I do not know sir. I heard that sometimes she did crochet work and laundry. In harder times, she may have had to beg, borrow or –

'Steal?' he suggested.

Reluctantly, I nodded.

'Was she 'fast', Mr Carter?' he asked abruptly.

'I never heard of anything like that.'

'Then why was she up and about at 2 am in the morning? Was she doing crochet work then?'

Made to wait until the laughter had subsided, I replied: 'I cannot say sir. I do not want to imagine.'

'From what you *have* already said it sounds very much as if things had taken a turn for the worse in the last few weeks of her life.'

'A month is long time on London's streets.'

'So I hear. Yet, if I have understood evidence from earlier correctly, she was not strictly homeless for the whole of that time.'

'I would think it very unlikely sir.'

'Do you have any idea, then, of where she had been living in the days leading up to her death?'

'Not really sir. I expect she would have stayed in lodgings when she could afford it; as for the rest, it would have been a bench in Itchy Park.'

As the coroner cocked an eyebrow one of the court officials intervened: 'I think that he may mean the churchyard of Christ Church, Spitalfields, sir.'

'The very same,' I confirmed.

'Thank you! Is it possible, then, that this is where she was heading when you followed her in your cab?'

'More than possible sir – likely, in fact, for that church is not a quarter of a mile from the spot where Mary and I last spoke.'

'I see. And where was that exactly?'

'It was on Thrawl Street – by then, we had moved on from the place of our first meeting and the area where she'd pulled her daft prank. She seemed hell-bent on carrying on, come what may, and despite her mood and her unfriendliness towards me I'd decided to escort her to wherever she was going – even if that be to make her bed under the stars. By that point she'd seemed to accept my presence and we crawled along together mostly in silence. Suddenly, I remembered it had been her birthday earlier that week for she had told me and made much of what she would do. For something to say, I enquired as to whether she had enjoyed her special day, to which she gave a horrid laugh. 'Special day? Don't give me that. I've had better in the spike!' 'Didn't you do much, then?' I asked her, already dreading her comeback. 'No I didn't! I never had two ha'pennies to rub together. Not so much as a quarter-gill wet my lips all day.' 'I'm sorry to hear it,' I consoled her. 'If I'd seen you about, you know I would've stood you a drink.' She shrugged. 'It don't matter, anyway. All that matters is my youngest's, in a few months' time.' 'Good,' I gently teased her, 'but with so many to remember I'm surprised you can keep up.' Well! What a mistake! My clumsy stab at humour certainly made its mark but not in the way I had intended, as Mary turned her gaze upon me and I saw a look in her eyes I'd never seen before. 'What did you just say?' she hissed at me. 'For your sake, Jeremiah, I hope to God I didn't hear you right!''

'Did you fear she might assault you?' the coroner asked.

'Possibly,' I answered truthfully. 'I told her it was nothing, that I was sorry and had spoken out of turn and to take no notice of me – but she'd have none of it and wouldn't let the matter lie. Eventually, I had to repeat what I had said.'

'And then?'

'Then her face turned ashen white and her voice fell to a whisper and Mary spoke the last words she was ever to say to me in this life. She said: 'Better to have spawned half-a-dozen than to have never fathered none.''

At this, the mirth in the gallery gave way to sharp intakes of breath and groans of misgiving, pierced by a sudden cry of 'Shame!''

'Silence in court!' the coroner shouted, banging his gavel. 'Mr Carter: why did not you previously speak of this in your statement to the police?'

'I don't recall sir.'

'And yet you choose to bring it up here today?'

'I think…I think it may have slipped my mind at the time.'

'Is that so? Then you must remedy this right away by telling us what happened next.'

'I'm not sure there is a great deal left to tell.'

'I will be the judge of that.'

'Mary left,' I complied, no longer caring of the opinion of others. 'The last I saw of her was her shadow disappearing down the Flowerydean.'

'What is that area like?'

I let out a snort as I tried to find some words.

'If I may say so sir,' put in the court official, 'it is a truly dreadful quarter.'

I raised my head, looked across at him and nodded.

'After that, I collected a few more fares; I cannot remember who or where it was we went. The last thing I recall is arriving back at the Yard, washing down my horse, walking home and falling into bed.'

'And that is all?' he pressed me, looking intently over his spectacles.

'Yes,' I replied.

'That is most unsatisfactory, Mr Carter.'

He made a brief note then turned to address the foreman. 'Does the jury have anything it wishes to ask?' After a consultation the man stood up to speak.

'We do, sir,' he declared, holding into his waistcoat. 'We would like to hear if the witness knows if Miss Nichols had any enemies or if he can think of any person who would wish to do her harm?'

'Mr Carter?'

'I know of no-one who would have wanted to hurt Mary,' I replied. 'As for her having enemies: I do not know the answer to that question.'

'Do you have enemies, Mr Carter?' the coroner asked me.

'Does not every man?' I said.

'Have you ever hit or threatened a woman?'

'Really sir!'

'Yet you said the two of you had had words –'

'I never touched her, I tell you! Never so much as laid a finger on her!'

'Now now, there is no need to get angry –'

'This is all unfair sir! I am innocent – and so is Mary! We never done anything wrong.'

'No-one here is implying that you did. I think that that will do,' he told the foreman.

Nodding, the man retook his seat.

'Mr Carter,' the coroner addressed me for the final time, 'before I call the next witness, can you think of anything else - anything at all - that may be of relevance to this case or is there anything further you wish to say?'

'Yes,' I answered huffily, 'there is: Mary was no saint, it's true, but she had hopes and dreams too, no different from the rest of us. She was a mother, a daughter and a sister-in-arms. Whatever monster did this to her is still out there. Something needs to be done.'

He put down his pen and sighed. 'Thank you, Mr Carter. You may go,' he said.

*

Over the course of the next few days I was to learn far more about the life of Mary Ann Nichols née Walker, blacksmith's daughter, once of Gunpowder Alley, than I had in the previous twelve months spent from time to time in her actual presence. It was impossible to pick up a penny paper, spy a news vendor or even roll past a poet's pitch without reading her name or catching a melancholy new refrain from the latest broadside ballad that would be the meal-ticket for many a canny chapman in the coming winter months.

I read dozens of lurid stories about her wicked, immoral life; pored over reams of reports investigating the 'shocking truth' of London's 'vile East End'; and caught headline after headline claiming to 'reveal' or 'exclusively expose' all manner of things, both great and small, once private and protected but now destined to be forever public – things from the recent past or, more often, Mary's hitherto secret history that had led to her tragic fall into a life of sin and shame, and which, it implied, helped make sense of her utterly senseless death.

I learnt the details of how she had deserted her husband and children some eight years previously, walking out on them for the final time after a blazing row that had started over her heavy drinking, she at first entering the Workhouse but soon choosing for herself the life of an Unfortunate; I read of her arrest in Trafalgar Square not long after I had met her, of her reputation, even then, as being amongst 'quite the lowest' of that raging sea of human misery; worst of all, I had to suffer accounts of the seemingly common knowledge (that was still news to me) of her sometimes being found so drunk and incapable that she had to be locked up for her own safety, allowed to leave only when she could prove to the custody sergeant that she could walk unsupported along a straight line and stand still on her own two feet – she, a houseless creature, who every officer knew would head immediately to the scene of her earlier downfall to resume her part in the waiting tragedy for which only the exact ending was not yet known.

In all of this, I noted that it was often her own people - the fruit of her loins, her dearly beloveds and still legally betrothed - who had taken their thirty pieces of silver to deny knowledge of and deflect all responsibility for the thing she had become. In my eyes, those who told of how her days were an endless quest for drink and her nights spent in bars or in doss-house kitchens were painting an unfair and incomplete picture of the Mary I had known. For she was - and had been to me - much more than all these things and not a week had passed when I reached the point where I had had my fill of seeing her memory dragged through the mud and her human frailties picked over like carrion bones with never the chance for a last loyal ally to reply or say 'Aye' or 'Nay'. Indeed, it took no time at all for a life that had been cut so cruelly short to be turned by some into a tale of warning, and by others made into a martyr's cause to the chant of which an angry drum could be beaten right up to the oppressor's door.

For it was Mary, and Mary alone, who had been on trial here, not he who had done all he could to defile her. Held up against an impossible standard and judged with indecent haste by the best authorities we could assemble, my only consolation lay in the blessed knowledge that in the mass of reported words, the pages of excited statements and the posters of juicy, twisted quotes, my own few words about her life were not deemed worthy of inclusion, when, as I knew, it might have been so different…for on exiting the courtroom and descending the institute steps, I had felt a hand squeeze my arm…

'You got a minute there, sir?' a young man in a billycock hat asked me chirpily.

'No,' I answered sharply. 'I have not.'

'It's the Daily News,' he continued. 'I'll make it worth your while!'

'I'm not interested and I do not want your money,' I told him, freeing myself from his grip and pushing my way through a ruck of reporters as they launched a barrage of questions at me: 'How bad was Polly, sir?; 'Do you think you saw him?; 'Who do YOU reckon did it?'

Reaching the road end, I was quick to hail a hansom, and, once inside, I drew breath and sunk low into my seat. As the cab rolled forward and I escaped the mob, I gazed out of the window at the passing buildings and the people standing in the street. I watched them all with growing wonderment and fear like a visitor to a foreign land instead of a man who prided himself on his intimate knowledge of this place's every rhythm, its weekly demands, daily business and hourly developments; keeper of a precious trove of accumulated knowledge of a population's latest hubs, secret loves, inexplicable manias, ingrained habits and incurable appetites.

Men in uniform enjoying a rare day's leave and clowning around to snare the interest of a young housemaid on an errand took on the shape of a pack of wolves in sheep's clothing as they laid their trap and eyed up their next kill. Grocery stores, victuallers, hosiers and ironmongers all became enticing Aladdin's caves, watched over by stout and unsmiling proprietors who stood at their doors or behind their counters like jealous, aproned dragons. Even the shoeblacks and errand boys roused my suspicions, their furtive eyes suggestive of a ring of local spies in the pay of some dark and occult agent.

Perhaps it was my sense of injustice at the tone of the inquest or my disappointment at my poor performance in the dock; perhaps it was the intrusions of day, so jarring to one now used to riding these roads under the sweet cover of night; or, most likely of all, perchance it was the alien sensation of for once being inside the cab and under the control of a nameless other. Whichever, by the time we had reached the end of Gracechurch Street then turned left at the Belgian consulate to take our place in the logjam on the long, gruelling approach to the river, I had drawn the curtain and shut out the rest of the world as my confidence in my memory crumbled and I scrambled to recover whatever I could from those last mislaid dregs of Friday's fatal dawn.

After leaving the Flowerydean with Mary Ann's callous jibe still ringing in my ears, where had I gone to next? South? No: north – for I can at least remember the stirring sight of a row of starched-white angels serving hot food and handing out bibles, even at that ungodly hour, to a boisterous brigade of Spitalfields's version of Judea's needy five thousand at the door of the East Provident soup kitchen. Awed by their example and chastised in equal measure by my own flagrant failure to always live up to my high and mighty ideals, I'd asked the Lord once more what I could do, and though I carried no loaves or fish with me and could not turn drain water into wine, there was surely some other act I could carry out on His behalf. How did Proverbs go again? *'Commit thy works unto the*

Lord and thy plans shall be established.' In my work, then, was where the mission lay.

I rode the streets - or I take it I must have done - for blurred snatches of the next three hours returned, with effort, reluctantly to me, as I'd searched for my allotted task in the worsening rain. I now recalled taking shelter under a railway bridge and speaking to a Dutch sailor who enquired with great concern about what had painted the night sky red; when I told him of the inferno he shook his head and scowled, declaring that all who sailed to London grew fat upon her wealth and that my city had just lost everything. Finding him too melodramatic for my mood, I'd ridden on, and sometime later must have dropped off another fare for I had a vision of pulling up outside the grey brick citadel of Whitechapel's Poor Law Bastille as it stood in the gloom like a tired but watchful mother awaiting her wayward child's return. Most painfully of all, I then retrieved the final excerpt of the night's forgotten business.

It had been after five o'clock for the sun's first rays had chased the clouds out of the sky. Here, on the cusp of day, in the deserted streets, was when I loved the city best, and I'd marked once again - as if anew, like every morning - how it was often at the fringe of things that fresh wonders were revealed and old truths reaffirmed. Guiding the hansom south along Baker's Row with a view to heading home, I'd fancied that I could see another vehicle approaching; pulling up in the haze, I'd shielded my eyes to try to see what it was that lumbered towards us with such ungainly movement and stuttering speed. At first, I thought I'd stumbled on a scene from olden times with a queen carried aloft her courtiers' shoulders in a weighty sedan chair – then, with sudden alarm, I made sense of the strange shape and knew I was witnessing the day's first labours for the men of East London's hand ambulance.

As it drew up beside me, two red-faced orderlies blew hard under the weight of their dead load, lowering the stretcher and sighing with relief as they tried to catch their breath.

'Good morning,' I greeted them softly.

'Is it?' panted the lead one, throwing me a black stare.

'Not for you, I'll avow. Who is it that you carry?' I asked, noticing the frill of a muddy skirt poking out from under the cover.

'Must you?' he snapped. 'Be very careful, sir, of what it is you wish to see!' with that reaching down and yanking back the cloth.

'Know her?' the other leered, relishing my reaction.

I shuddered, shook my head and looked away.

'Nor we – but she is only a tart they say and no great loss-...though I doubt even she deserved to die that way.'

'What about you? You just starting?' his partner asked, and I knew he was eyeing up the hansom in the role of a temporary hearse.

'I have just finished,' I muttered, 'and am driving home.'

'Lucky you! We will be stuck with her for many hours. Don't let her spoil your sleep.'

'I will try,' I said.

I watched as they lifted the litter and bore her on to some lowly brick shed or cold police mortuary, to be stripped, labelled, photographed and sliced open, before being stitched up, hastily wrapped in cheap sacking and flung, minus all ceremony, into a pauper's grave.

*

After riding back to Bermondsey and stabling Belle I'd left the yard and walked the few hundred yards home to my foxhole with the warming kiss of the rising sun on my back. Halfway down Albert Street I'd come to the familiar front door and on going inside had paused outside the parlour before deciding instead to hang my wet cloak over a chair in the hall. Heading upstairs, I'd entered my room and stood at her side of the empty bed which had, I confess, of late, turned into something of a shrine. Beside the relics of such a beautiful life, what could that other woman's fate really mean to me?

Led by the lingering suspicion that all such persons brought their end upon themselves and confronted by the sight of the love and hate that can dwell in a single human heart, the maimed body on the handcart was proof once more that man and woman, made equal in God's sight, can never really be, and that, in this world, a woman without a husband will never come to any good; for the eyes that had stared up at me and refused to leave my head as I climbed into bed had not belonged to just a tart or a fallen stranger but were those of my friend poor bloody Mary, alias Polly, also known as Mary Ann.

6

A Gladstone Bag

If Southwark's main parish poorhouse is rightly feared then London's hospital for the insane possesses all the appeal of a beautified corpse. Always worth a try for a pick-up in the small hours of the night, one man's downfall is at once another man's opening and with so many new comings and goings - nurses, relatives, superintendents with new patients, the public and the press - it is an irresistible draw for the concerned and the curious, the one forever on the lookout for signs of abuse or neglect to bolster their campaigns for reform; the other, paying spectators of the saddest form of human tragedy, interested only in finding another level of existence more woebegone than their own. When we near, though, I find its gates shut and its patrolling wardens nowhere to be seen as if the entire operation has been put under lockdown and something else apart from the bedlam is being kept cooped-up inside.

Disappointed, I leave its misty grounds and haunting night music behind us and continue on north but after a mile or more of trawling for custom I have not succeeded in getting anyone to bite. The streets of the south shore are unnaturally quiet but I pinpoint my real problem when I approach the crossing at Blackfriars and the bridge keeper frantically signals to me to re-illuminate my lights. As we traverse the river the whole vehicle judders as one of its wheels drops into a pothole. Cursing my luck, I make the other side and steer the cab into a rest spot to survey the extent of the damage and to investigate the source of a metallic clashing noise like a mechanism or part has become dislodged.

My initial inspection reveals nothing of major worry, all spokes, springs and levers present and correct. Mercifully, it seems as though the cab has escaped with knocks only – but just as I'm checking the axle I notice the end of an object poking out from the rack underneath the passenger seat. Puzzled, I discover that it is the handle of a leather bag, the kind that is typically carried by a locum or surgeon and sometimes called a 'Gladstone'. My first reaction is that it must have been left by an absent-minded fare and that I shall have to hand it in to the Yard upon completion of my shift; but as I lift it out to see if I can garner any clues as to its owner, its sheer weight and the ringing of steel divulge that its contents are anything but your usual hand luggage.

Fastened at the top with a lanyard tied in a sailor's knot, inside it I find a motley collection of instruments, tools and sharps. There are awls, forceps, clips and clamps, a hacksaw, hammer and a chisel; a burin, a pair of opera glasses, a tidal clock, spirit gum and a cleaver. In amongst them all are a whetstone, a dirty rag, two bottles of ink, a phial of rat poison and a half-empty bottle of rum. This jumble must needs belong to a jack-of-all-trades. Mostly, though, there are knives. Knives for slicing, knives for dicing. Knives for cutting, knives for carving. Knives for shearing, knives for smearing. Knives for killing.

I try to recall any patron who may have brought the bag on board but no obvious candidate springs to mind – queerer still, it appears to have been deliberately stored there or sequestered in the last few days, resting upon a fresh copy of a popular illustrated newssheet published less than a week ago. I think about going in search of a bobby on the beat or else dropping it into the bottom of the Thames but both actions, I realize, risk casting aspersions upon myself, and I have no wish to squander a few hours' pay by spending the rest of the night pleading my ignorance behind a wooden table in Bow.

A once-remembered music - most alien of all in the heart of London - breaks its way into my musing: the sound of free-running water. The Fleet, or a pale shadow of it, one of this place's ancient rivers, spills its contents into the lap of the great Mother via a conduit beneath Blackfriars Bridge. Once so pure as to be made into the mead brewed by the brotherhood after whom the area is named, it is now a river rank, choked, a disease-ridden abomination, holy water become a sewer. Blocked, built over, diverted and drained, centuries of misuse have seen to it that most of its lower streams have dried up out of all knowledge, its glorious past as forgotten as the people it used to feed, doughty folk of a class like me brought up to love their mothers and always eat their greens.

First rising in Hampstead, Belle and I have inadvertently followed its tortured course from its headwaters on the Heath to its dribbling mouth, less a tribute than a tired and token offering to a city that no longer heeds it. I wonder what the order of devout men who once tended their kitchen gardens along its green and verdant banks would make of it now and the flotsam and jetsam it collects, its putrid condition reflecting the state of faith and its shallow channel treated as an ever-willing accessory to all our fair and foul designs. Yet in spite of everything still it persists and for those who know where to stop and listen it can be heard in times of spate through a grate or a mossy culvert as if whispering to us that it is still here, where it always was, and where it ever shall be once our selfish labours fail, our godless society fades and our doomed kind withers and returns to dust.

The skies have cleared again and the image of the waxing moon floats in the silent Thames, the point in the river where the tide turns. I look at the bag and this time notice some writing on the outer leather picked out by the soft moonlight. It is a signature, painted on by hand and partly worn away:

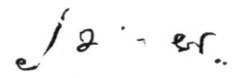

85

Visible alongside it is some kind of symbol or emblem – a butterfly, or possibly a moth, making me wonder if the bag is the property of a scientist or an avid specimen collector. Rifling through it once more to test my theory, I pull out a large curved blade. An attempt has been made to wipe it clean yet its handle is still stained with clumps of dried blood. I do not like the feel of this at all and as I deliberate over what to do a sudden cough behind me makes me peer over my shoulder.

'Help an ex-sailor and spare some change, guv'nor.'

Much as I normally would, this is neither the time nor the place.

'I'm sorry but I'm busy just now.'

'No doubting that, guv'nor, no doubting that at all…but not so busy, surely, as to ignore the plight of an old war hero who finds himself down on his luck?'

It is no use, so I stop what I am doing and rake around in my pocket. I find him a few coppers and as he holds out his hand I notice a tattoo of a bird on the inside of his wrist – a seafaring insignia or more likely a memento of a quick-fire visit to port.

'Much obliged,' he wheezes, as he counts the money then turns his back and lets out an ear-piercing whistle.

In seconds I find myself cornered by a small army of paupers who have emerged from the arches of the bridge. They beseech me for more brass, slyly tugging at my clothing and I feel a hand rifling for my purse. One even starts to worry Belle for any pickings and now a line has definitely been crossed.

'Back off!' I warn them. 'Touch her again and I'll – '

'You'll do what?' one of them bares his feral teeth, to a collective hacking of lungs.

I reach carefully behind me.

'Hello! What have you got there, chief?' one of them cranes his neck as I inch my hand forward.

'Holy mackerel!'

'It's the Knife!' another yells. 'Run for your lives!'

Like rats on a sinking ship the men scatter, the gleaming crescent of the razor-sharp sickle a primal hex as potent as the heavenly body above us. Calamity averted for the present, I resolve to keep the bag by my side until such time as someone reclaims it. After all, I have nothing to hide and, if questioned, can reasonably argue that the specialist items within are highly unlikely to be my own, their more lethal uses a sleeping partner providing a man with a welcome degree of protection. Taking the Gladstone up to my seat, without further ado we ride on and make for Farringdon Street.

My drought finally ends when a man dressed in foreign garb walks out right in front of the hansom, forcing me to brake.

'Oi! Watch where you're going there!' I hector him.

In reply, he put his hands together and bows.

He has all the appearance of a young Lascar and sports their typical outlandish attire: his richly embroidered ivory coat reaches to just below his knee covering tight-fitting pants and pointed slippers adorned in green and white corals; a full beard droops over his high collar above which he wears a bejewelled head robe, the whole finished off with a thick tartan sash and a ceremonial dagger hanging from his waist.

Many of my colleagues outright decline to have one in the cab but most are not the lazy starvelings they are often made out to be and I never found them any trouble. This one's quaint costume lends him more the look of a maharaja than castaway merchant crew and as he puffs on a cigar I cannot picture him sharing three-to-a-bed in the Strangers' Home or running up and down the rigging, the ropes between his toes and a dab hand in laying the mainsail aloft. These types are portrayed as not speaking a word of the Queen's - or else just about enough to get the things they want - but this one addresses me in near-perfect English, living proof both of his caste and the far-reaching power of our people.

'A thousand apologies! I thought you had missed me.'

'Fat chance of that!'

The crass jibe, thankfully, is lost in translation, as he holds up a shiny florin and hands me a letter of introduction addressed to a titled recipient.

I frown: it is obvious that the building named will now be closed for whatever business he can possibly have there. I tell him as much but he smiles as if humouring my stupidity and politely nods his head.

'Just so. I beg that you take me anyway. You will do me a great favour.'

He has had fair warning and if he wants to waste his money then that is up to him – ours not to reason why.

'Very well, sir,' I sigh. 'Exactly as you wish.'

'Thank you. I am forever in your debt – though I fear I am late already.'

'Fret not,' I tell him. 'You're in safe hands now. I'll have you there tout de suit.'

Islington beckons and as we head north again we drive through the area that was once the stomping ground of my father, collector of the night soil. How life has changed since those naïve days when the biggest challenge facing him was a collapsed drain, a blocked sewer or a leaching cesspool. Though it is a known fact that the roads of yesteryear were not worthy of the name, riven scars ankle deep in mire, his nightly round was still a straightforward one in comparison with the difficulties I am expected to endure. Confounded by a host of rules and regulations and taxed to kingdom come, I am also asked to familiarise myself with the ways and strange customs of every nationality, colour and creed.

In my own lifetime the face of the capital has altered beyond all recognition, changing at a pace and moving in a direction never previously imagined. The old lines on which our lives were laid are fast disappearing and the docks awash with people of every shade - red faces, yellow and brown - so that the native Londoner whose work takes him there soon finds himself an outsider in his own town. It is true that many are loyal subjects of the Empire and amongst those who have settled here their children look, for the most part, healthy and comfortably dressed – yet what do we really know of them and their secretly held beliefs? When it comes to these murders it need hardly be said that no Englishman is capable of such a deed. Whilst a woman always lies at the heart of these matters - inspiring lust, jealousy or revenge - from what I hear these recent outrages are less crimes of passion than part of some savage religious ritual. A cab driver's work brings him into contact with every incarnation of humankind, so who knows what man or monster might have been pulled along by this very hansom…and though my fare sits as peacefully as a gold Buddha below me, maybe there is more to that deadly weapon of his than pure ceremony or traditional costume.

I look at Belle and my eyes pore over her lustrous coat as she plunges into a haze of sea-coal smoke like a snowflake amidst a shower of cinders. Since my return she is the one thing that has kept me sane and I know I would be lost without her. Yet as I pay her closer attention I ask myself how well I really understand her. If, for argument's sake, we say that horse has lived in this land for several thousand years, then in the ups and downs of its improbable journey these modern times are less a chapter than a trivial footnote. It is a simple fact that I can only tell a part of her tale – the bit that is relevant to me. Her wild and spirited race have had to adapt to survive, be loyal and show deep courage in the face of the tests we set them; yet in truth does 'loyal' really mean 'cowed', and is their so-called 'courage' simply the Hobson's choice of a creature that finds itself trapped? Maybe the high-pitched whinny that she gives on sight of me is no more loving than the learnt bark of the chained guard dog that slavers and bays for its tripe…and if that be so, then Lord forgive me for my whole life story is a sham and I worry I might just go mad.

I start to notice now that she is gnawing on the bit, a fault of hers which only usually rears its head when something has made her skittish. As we continue, her performance worsens as she yanks petulantly at the reins and drags her hind hooves as if refusing to carry on. In the end, I have no choice but to pull up at the roadside and get out to see if I can calm her down.

Her mouth is foaming so I gently pull out the bridle piece, all the while stroking her head and seeking to give her comfort. I see that we have halted opposite a vast, cavernous warehouse, the main entrance to the open meat market at Smithfield. In just a few hours' time the entire concourse with be heaving with racks of carcasses for sale; butchers and wholesalers will soon rub crimson elbows in the bar of The Slaughtered Lamb. Perhaps this, then, is the reason behind the mare's behaviour: is it possible that she rebels at the stench of flesh – or does an intuitive sense of the violent demise of her distant kin somehow linger in the air?

For animals, let me tell you, are not at all like human beings. Take a beast, lock it in a cage, keep it in cramped, filthy, degrading conditions; beat, berate, neglect and ignore it; truss it and tether it then suddenly set it loose only to lead it to its death, and at the end of its whole painful, pointless existence, as it heads to the waiting blade, it will crave one single, solitary thing above all else: more life. My own beloved grey who under my childhood roof was ever put on a pedestal and held up as the epitome of all beauty, honesty and grace, has known precious little of the betrayal of men but even I, her one true master, sometimes toil to coax her into the black pit of immorality London has become, nothing her forebears endured in the vagaries of battle or that she herself has experienced in her many long years of service preparing her for the sights, sounds and smells she must encounter in these least handsome of hansom times.

Turning to my passenger to express my sincere regret for the delay, I flinch as I am met by a stomach-churning sight: the Lascar has swathed himself from head to toe in a plain dark cloth and as he holds up his left palm, with his right he wields the dagger and carves the sign of the Evil Eye into his naked skin. He does not waver in the act and extends his arm outwards as if trying to ward off a near or present danger, and if he is really a prince then the fable is false for his blood is not blue but runs as red as ours. I elect to say nothing, tidy up the mare, and, satisfied that she is ready again, recommence our curious ride.

For the first time tonight the temperature has started to plummet and this, in tandem with a drop in the wind, does not help in clearing the dense and fetid vapour. By the time we arrive at our illustrious destination the square is shrouded in an orange fog, our way lit only by a pair of burning braziers set outside the door of the ornate townhouse. Whilst all the other residences lie in darkness, a lamp flickers inside ours. I feel the hansom lighten and hear padded footsteps receding and, in what can only be a trick of the light, a valet appears who holds a brief conversation at the empty threshold before the door swings further open then rapidly slams shut as if a guest has just been admitted.

Befuddled, I jump down and peer into the cab to find the trap deserted and my exotic fare nowhere to be seen, the only proof that he was not a figment of my fancy the shiny florin and a silver amulet left upon the seat. Examining the charm and unsure if it is meant as a tip or has, more likely, slipped out of his pocket, I opt for caution, hasten over and knock on the door. After a short delay, the same man answers.

He looks me up and down, his top lip curling slightly. 'Yes? Can I help you, sir?' he asks, in his blunt, buttoned-up manner.

'I hope you can,' I reply unperturbed. 'That man you just let in – he left this inside my cab. I wasn't sure if –'

'A *man*, sir?'

'Yes. Just a few moments ago. You must surely...' my voice trailing off as over his shoulder I observe quite a soiree taking place in the inner sanctum of the house: a row of blindfolded servants stand holding loaded trays of drinks, kept in good line by the hissed directives of a pernickety butler, his tense demeanour in sharp contrast with those he is paid to serve, the brazen lechery and unseemly conduct of many of the assembled guests all the more galling as I realize that I am in the presence of some of the most famous faces and widely-celebrated names in the land.

'Is there a problem, sir?' the waiting valet enquires of me in withering tones.

'No,' I start. 'I'm quite alright, thank you. Pray tell me: in the room back there, I thought I recognised –'

'I'm sure that I'm not at liberty to say.'

'Yes, of course,' I weakly yield.

'Moreover,' he continues, seeking to press home his advantage, 'if I may be so bold, sir, I'm sure that whoever I just 'let in' - if indeed I did so - would not be in the habit of accidentally leaving luggage, or any other object for that matter, in the trust and care of a man like you. If, I may be so bold.'

'A man like me?'

He does not flinch. 'Sir.'

Before I can ask him what he means there is a loud crash from above and the chandelier lights in the hallway dim and flicker to collective 'oohs' and 'aahs', a ripple of excitement running through the room as everyone turns to look, mesmerised by the sight of the now bewigged Lascar descending the stair arm in arm with a beautiful consort. At this, a footman taps the valet's shoulder and as he scurries off I continue to watch proceedings until a passing maid notices the open door and slams it in my face.

Returning to the cab, placing the charm around my neck then pocketing the coinage, I know better than to pry further, leaving my fare's fate in the hands of my betters. Dusky brother or dark imposter of the subcontinent, I feel sure I will not see him again tonight – a situation with which I am most at ease as I retake my pew and give the waiting Belle the old *'Ee-aye! a' time we were away!'*

My luck is in again as the next job is not slow in forthcoming. Hurrying out from the railed gardens in the middle of the square, a youngish fellow of about my age chases us down just as we are primed to canter off.

'Driver!' he shouts out. 'Driver! Just a tick!'; I dutifully answer the call.

His eyes are bleary and his shirt and trousers are covered with grass as if he has made his nest beneath a hedge but as I give him the quick once-over he does not exhibit the signs of the truly down-at-heel, having at least shoes and socks, a clean-shaven jaw and full cheeks not wanting for soap or sustenance; indeed, he treats me to a portion of his life story before I can independently assess him.

'What a chance!' he croons. 'The first good news I've had today. Oh, someone throw a crumb of hope to poor Jacob MacIver! It's just like this, see: I set out early doors - as usual - for my long stint at the foundry but on getting there an irate crowd had mustered at the gate so I had it all on just to push my way forwards. Bumping into my pal, he tells me to look alive and go inside to

92

retrieve what possessions I may. When I asked him why, he says: 'Ain't you heard? We've only been turned off!' Well! I thought my life had ended and just like that I find myself out on my ear. Fifteen years I've been stuck in that horrible furnace and see what they've gone and done to me! I took off to the nearest pot-house, got sozzled and there I've stayed all day. In the end, though, I says to myself, 'Jacob, it's time to face the music,' but on my way home I got weary like and in mooching about here it struck me how pleasant the gardens looked and I decided to have forty winks. The next thing I know I peel my eyes open to the funniest thing I've ever seen: a set of clothes, Eastern they looked, floating their way through the fog into one of the swell houses. I'd be lying if I said I didn't think I was still dreaming…but then your cab rolled by and I saw my chance. Thank God you stopped! I've got a hell of a lot of explaining to do to the missus once I'm back… she'll be on pins trying to occupy the young one – and another on the way! Oh mister, just take me straight there won't you, for all I want now is to see their loving faces!'

It is some speech, this man's, but unless he is an actor every part of his unhappy tale seems to ring true. He is one of us, the working poor, forever on the brink, and I can see that his sudden dismissal has shaken him to the core, so is it any wonder he dreaded returning home to break the news to his tearful wife as she cradled their mewling child? I can tell, too, from his unsteady gait that he is still more than half-seas over – though to his credit he has made a good fist of seeming to have sobered up.

His wish is my command and he clumsily clambers in, slumping down and leaning his head against the glass. The eyes start to roll so before his lights go out I ask him where he wants to be, catching the word 'Olborn' to at least set us on our way.

It is to there then that we head: a bustling district of rowdy taverns and mean tenements, not two miles as the crow flies but more as the mare gallops. Keeping to the banks of the canal, now sadly in decline, we follow a waterway which in its heyday transported coal and other goods up and down the land. In time, though, this lucrative trade was lost to the new railways and the clogged channel left behind by the ever-turning wheel of progress. If one thing can be said about this city it's that it never rests on its laurels; just as freight trains overtook the barges, so did cabs usurp the passenger boats. Maybe one day, too, the horse will be replaced and Peter's Yard will find its days numbered and it will be my turn to feel aggrieved – though precisely what kind of contraption could compete with Belle, your guess is as good as mine.

The various happenings of the night are beginning to take their toll and for the first time I myself feel a little tired. It is no use bleating though and there is nothing for it but to carry on. My mind turns again to my father and the only life he ever knew. I may have been overhasty in my casual dismissal of his pains.

Looking back, my parents' time was no bed of roses either, the two of them forced into living separate lives as creatures of the dark and light: he, on the same treadmill from dusk till dawn so ingrained in me now; she, ever fretful and alone in the coldest hours so that oftentimes my bedtime story was read to me by the other Father in whom mother did frequently confide, the last sight I saw as I slipped into sleep the priest's retreating surplice.

Was it this, then, that lay at the root of Joseph Carter's vexation? Capable yet thwarted by a lack of self-belief, industrious yet sucked deeper by the day into the mire, he watched and withered as I grew to be the self-made man he was destined not to be. How hollow those sermons we sat and listened to must have sounded that spoke of the dignity of labour, the godliness of work. In the prime of life his life was never his own, and of all familiar things his family most unfamiliar of all, his wife's profile seen more in a locket than by the fireside and time with his one begotten son ever sacrificed on the altar of his self-respect.

I suppose that, for all my airs and graces, in my own way I am a collector of the night soil, rounding up the spoil and detritus of our daily existence and carting it away like a shameful secret before the advent of each new morning.

Each of us, too, has our own Gladstone bag to carry, laden with hopes, ambitions and desires. Some are bountifully provisioned, crammed with all of the materials required to plan, build and defend a realm. Others are less well-filled, handed down with but a few meagre items, made for men who Fate has tasked to be more resourceful and who must bend and twist each instrument to their will – not to shape a dynasty but to dismantle one. Such unfavoured sons must learn to make do and mend, sometimes after a fight, constantly kept down and beaten at last by those fatal factors that - notwithstanding ability and endeavour - ultimately decide how a man is to sit astride his horse.

For some, to be a knight; for others, a nightsoilman.

An Upstairs Room

In my thirst for knowledge after my second coming I discovered much I never knew about the power of words. As a youngster I had hung onto every syllable spoken at the lectern and my home bible studies had introduced me to some of the greatest passages ever written, yet I still grew to be a man who lived and worked with eyes shut and moved amongst a harried people who 'see no Visions in the darksome air.' My own awakening was to come much later and in the unlikeliest of places – but once Father Cronin had led me through the magic door I learnt that simple words, properly wrought, could not just be a channel for my peace but in my ongoing travails in the land of the living also help me to commune with the dead.

It all began, as I have said, when my earthly saviour found me rolling a great boulder up the steep and everlasting slopes of Purgatory. There, punished for my avarice and in the once-cherished company of complaining clergymen, cardinals and popes, I sweated and sank in the scorching ash under the immense load of my own human greed. My gaze fixed on the summit, I pushed and pressed my terrible burden until I could push and press no more, at last losing my grip and watching powerlessly as it bumped its way down the mountain, knocking all souls and obstacles out of its path before making the edge and plunging forever into the mouth of the fathomless abyss.

In the endless day of that infinite desert of desolation, remorse quickly wrapped its tendrils round me and bitter were the ground waters that sustained me under the cruel heat of an invisible sun, but the red pilgrim who had wandered far to find me cleared the weeds from my feet and put balm on my sores and sought to mend me with his softly spoken words of insight. To his shadow I clung as a new-born kid trails behind its mother, following him into vile valleys and along dismal dust roads and traipsing over stony and broken lands till even he wearied and sat down and tugged fretfully at his beard. Time stood still - if such a place has such a thing as time - and I know not how, or when, but all at once I felt the air sharpen and a veil of dew kissed my weather-beaten face and looking up I discovered my guide had gone and that I was standing at the entrance to a darkened wood.

Exploring its dells and thickets for what seemed like aeons with no sign of any other living thing, I eventually came across a woman standing in a glade who started to sing then sighed and shook her head as if in self-reproach as she combed the knots out of her waterfall of hair. I approached her cautiously and fancied I had once known her but could not recognise her face or remember her name. Her age I could not guess but she was both youthful and sage, and her locks were not so much grey as altogether colourless and as she noticed me a coy smile played faintly around her lips. Addressing me, she said: 'So you have come at last. Well met! You seek out that which is not here. I was told of your wife's passing, as I am of all of my children. I have no news to impart and cannot lighten your heart but knowledge is not always what it seems and just as there are things to come that have always been, so what is now is already past. Yet why should a man not read the page of his own destiny if it is already writ in the Book? Here, take this, and if you wish to know yourself better, taste of it as you will…' and with this she handed me a piece of rotten fruit she had lifted from the forest floor – and suddenly I knew that the dying wood with its hoary and infested boughs had once been home to a beautiful garden, full of birdsong and blossom and bounded by a plentiful orchard. Her eyes widened as I raised the morsel to my lips – and then I looked at the spot whence the food had come and saw that the ground was choked with weeds and littered with blunted tools and tree roots that roiled with venomous vipers that attacked each other and swallowed their own tails, and I understood, too, that she was now quite as barren as the soil she pointlessly worked. I hesit-

97

ated and in an instant her face contorted with pain and I dropped the fruit and ran.

Reaching the plantation's edge as I fled from the henchmen that the Son of the Morning had set upon me, I spied a rocky mount and crawled inside a hollow cairn and fell into restless slumber. In between sleep and wakefulness I was joined by another who had also been 'long abroad' and as we spoke he enquired of my heart's desire; when I told him, he replied that he knew of a secret way that led to the place where I wished to be and a bargain was struck that he would take me there and tell me how to pass unknown, if in return I sent others down in my stead that he 'not long be deprived of company'.

'But mind!' he warned me, having trod the same path himself, 'those who watch it take no prisoners – and mark well the Poet who said:

'Subtle he needs must be, who could seduce Angels.'

So together we hatched a glorious deceit that I might steal into Heaven.

The stair, my companion told me, would be well-guarded and they would be sure to check me against the great list. The only way through, then, was to adopt the guise of another: one already dead but unable to attest his own name. He put his mouth close to my ear as he made his suggestion and I recoiled both at his breath and the gist of his words.

'I cannot do it,' I informed him.

'Yet you must,' he countered. 'Alas, there is no other choice.'

'Then I turn back.'

'And risk never seeing her again?'

Torn between the draw of flesh on flesh and what was right and wrong, but no equal to his clever counsel and honeyed words, I took his lead as we hacked through scrub and thorns and sought to evade the attentions of rabid beasts until midway along a cleft he halted, sniffed the reek and closely studied the face of a towering cliff.

'Ha!' he exclaimed and pointed in triumph to a trail of tiny pink star-shaped flowers growing out of the naked rock.

Fain to believe that a thing so pure and delicate could thrive in this miasma, I stared back in amazement as he motioned to give me a foot-up up the cliff face, directing me to 'Go!' Yet as I baulked at the idea of tackling such an obstacle, I found that the rock possessed a special purchase and that by keeping to the course of the creeping herb I was guided to a series of natural handholds and soon had scaled a dizzying height to the safety of a narrow ledge. Shouting down to ask him where to make for next, the valley floor was obscured by spirals of steam and the answer - if it was he who gave it - reverberated all around the gorge without ever taking form. Looking up I saw nothing but a sprig of old heather dangling just within my reach and left with little choice I made a grab for it and pulled and clawed my way up like a lizard, scrambling on until at last the slope eased and I reached a rustic wooden platform built into a recess in the mountain wall.

Two angels clad in armour helped me up and led me to a bench where others sat. Pressing a sponge to my lips they asked for my name and when I gave them the one agreed upon I knew I had committed a great sin. Stiff in my seat, the doleful minutes turned to hours as they turned the pages of a hefty tome, meticulously checking each record and debating every entry in a musical tongue I had never previously heard but wholly understood. In the end, one summoned me over, drew his sword and regarded me with his bright and terrible eye before informing me that I was free to go on.

Now serene, he said, 'We had some trouble finding you, for you have taken your time in getting here…yet not all of those who are listed make it this far so it is better to be late than never.'

'Is it much further?' I asked him.

'Further?' he echoed. 'I tell you that you have but reached the first level and the stage posts are as many as rungs on a belfry ladder. We have never counted them but of all of a man's labours this is surely amongst the lightest.'

'Here,' said the other, handing me a gourd of water, 'the next

99

step is just behind that rock. Rest first if you wish for once you have started there is no turning back...' – yet when I showed them I desired to depart at once they waved me forward and bid me 'Godspeed!"

Buoyed by the triumph of our simple ruse, I was soon in motion and undaunted by the prospect of a long climb, eager also to put some altitude between us lest our plot come to unravel. After my earlier feats, tackling the winding stair seemed easy: some parts of it were made of stone, some carved from marble, other sections fashioned from branches and vines, so that I chirped to the firmament like a lark released as I scaled the sacred highway.

To begin with, I came across the odd fellow journeyman and we congratulated ourselves on our progress and the glories to come; yet with every level I completed so the path quietened, the rest stops grew fewer and I fell into morbid silence. Each upward step came more reluctantly than the last and as I struggled to breathe I bemoaned the memory of the smiling protagonist who had put me up to such folly. Blinded by a brilliant light above me and gazing across a carpet of cloud, my head reeled and after a false turn I found myself cragfast and knew that I could do nothing more, wondering how long it might be as I clung weakly to the mountainside before I finally closed my eyes and commended my spirit into His hands...

She waited in the company of a divine assembly planning to gently chide me for leaving her alone that day but on first sight of me she spread her wings, swooped down and bore me away to some preposterous fir-clad pinnacle where we fell, sobbing, into each other's arms. Like Persephone, from Pandemonium via Chaos and the Cosmos up to the gates of Heaven itself, I had passed through earth, air, fire and water, transported from the edge of the void to heights beyond all human ecstasy, so there without further thought or deed I lounged and loved for a year and a day in the sweet rapture of that blissful bower.

Sanctified by her caress and anointed by her kiss, in time I attained a lightness of being that possessed every mortal mariner whose sketchy star map had landed him there. Only once I had recovered did she think it prudent to hold a mirror to my face. I saw then, as had she, how low I must have stooped and she recalled her shock at the stranded figure she had rescued from the rock, saying, 'You seemed to me more like a lost prophet of old than my long-lamented horseman. I was afraid I was mistaken or had gone delirious – yet I would trace your shadow across the tablet of history and know your shape in an exodus of forty thousand souls.'

But for all the freedom and ease of our connubial aerie, I knew my stint in Paradise could not last forever for my earthly days had not yet been accounted for in full and so the hour came when the Archangel Michael finally penetrated my guise. Raining his fury on our haven even whilst we slept, he spared none of our coterie and brushed all resistance aside so that the heavenly minstrels threw away their instruments and even Alice shrank from me when she learnt the truth of what I had done. Casting me down to never return until such time as 'Death and Judgement restore me', he banished me from the celestial sphere and as I fell into nothingness shadow consumed me, the sky shook and all horizons vanished.

My next consciousness was of the sound of nervous laughter and a crowd of people watching me. Opening my eyes, I found myself curled up on the cobbles and as I got to my feet I instinctively shook off my wings just as a serpent sheds its skin. Folk cried out in alarm and some retreated as they do from the roving leper and though I looked only for alms and meant no harm I feared I might be lynched. Slipping away, I passed by scenes not unknown to me yet every detail was newly vivid and strange as if I had previously viewed the ordinary world like a story read in stained glass; whereas once were only people going about their business, now all I could see were streets crammed with those already marked out for their fate. As I mixed again with men - the new-born and the damned - want was everywhere and I saw no hopeful vistas, only God's grand design disarranged and, aye, all darkness visible. Pained by the lives lain in ruins on every corner, my mind was beset by questions, questions – questions I needed to ask: if God be good and all-powerful then in the face of such sorrow why did He not see fit to intervene? Did He not pale to witness the state of His greatest creation and if evil endure too then who created it if not He, who is the author of all things?

In search of answers, I turned to a newer set of doctrine that spoke a dissenting language, preaching that Man should not expect to find holiness anywhere but rather 'build a Heaven in Hell's despair.' It was naught but blind faith and a waste of the powers given to us by God to wring our hands and wait for divine intervention – better to step outside and bring the gospel into being than live a life of passive virtue. The whole universe could be found in a grain of sand - perhaps, in a single name - and the war for Jerusalem was not to be fought on a distant plane but right here on Planet Earth. All that remained was for Man to decide what kind of witness he would be.

Rejuvenated and with new fire in my belly, I resolved to wage my own crusade in the holy land of my fathers in the only way I knew how, my road leading me back to the wholesome stench of Peter's Yard as I came face-to-face with my never-forgotten charger. As I rubbed her ears, I remembered how in the haze of one youthful summer we had started out together, an unbreakable bond forged between us as we found our feet and learned the tricks of our trade; now, Belle and I had a different mission and darkness itself would be my muse as we commenced our nightly round of the blasphemous city to share the news of God's undying Love and to dispense His mystical Justice.

*

In the Stygian gloom that regularly grips the metropolis even a careful man can get waylaid or disappear, so I am gladdened when after a ride of twenty minutes the shape of High Holborn greets my eye. Though much of the rest of London is away to bed, this area is still very much alive and in the garish light thrown out from the windows of its gin palaces there is more than enough colour and gaiety to purge the brooding mind. The narrow pavements are

103

teeming with drunken revellers and every known depravity prac-tised in the solid shadows cast by the great Inns of Court – and yet, for the wistful heart, it is hard not to be taken in by its cheap and lurid charms or by the chorus of lusty voices released into earshot each time a saloon door swings open:

> *'Champagne Charlie is my name,*
> *Good for any game at night, my boys,*
> *good for any game at night...'*

Reaching the junction of New Street, Shoe Lane and the via-duct, I am in need of further instruction and refreshment, so I kill two birds with one stone by dropping a hand and steering the cab up to the threshold of a galleried coach house. I have not heard so much as a peep from my latest consignment since we left the back-waters of Canonbury behind us; pulling up, I step down and peer inside to find him slumped and insensible in his seat, all vigour and expression seemingly extinguished from his face. For a moment I panic and give him a sharp jab in the ribs but a splutter and groan allay my worst fears as he rolls onto his side and nestles in as if settling down for the duration.

Happy to leave him for the time being I set the chocks and take a slurp and splash my face at the public wellhead. To the left is a stone crib, both facilities provided and maintained by the Metro-politan Drinking Fountain and Cattle Trough Association in the interests of all livestock and their men. On occasion, I have even come across a box of provender here, such small anonymous acts of kindness helping keep the cartwheels turning. Tonight, though, Belle must settle for a simple pail of 'fresh' and as I wait for her and survey the raucous neighbourhood, I see that chance has brought me to within spitting distance of the onetime ivory tower of the tragic Boy Poet of Gray's Inn. Seized by a sudden impulse, I look about me; spying the figure of a woman loitering near to the adjacent tavern, I try to make her acquaintance...

'I say, missy!'

'Who? Me?' she starts.

'Yes – you there! Are you free?'

'Do I look it?' she scoffs, keeping to the brightly-lit entrance-way.

'I'm guessing that you are. How do you fancy earning yourself a penny or two?'

'Depends what for,' she eyes me suspiciously.

'Oh, don't be afeard – it's nothing too taxing. Come here and I'll show you what's what.'

'I will not! Who are you, anyway?'

'Just a working man who needs a favour.'

'Aye, right! And I'm the Virgin Mary.'

I sigh inwardly and try a new tack. 'How about I stand you a jar: anything you like. You can get yourself your favourite tipple.'

She visibly swithers. 'What do you really want?'

'I want nothing.'

'Pull the other one!'

'No, honestly. You have me all wrong.'

'I tell you what, then: come into the warmth for a few minutes and let me have a good gander at you.'

'I'm sorry, I don't have the time. Just be done with it will you and pick your poison…'

'No!'

'You won't help me, then?'

She shakes her head. 'I answers only to my other half…on the days when he's compos mentis. These streets ain't safe no more. I could have you arrested. Go on and be on your way!'

It is clear I am getting nowhere but roused by the commotion another female's silhouette appears at the balcony of the coach house.

'Hey – you lot! What's all this racket about? My customers are trying to sleep up here!'

'It's nothing, Rosie. I was just asking this gentleman to leave.'

'Were you now? Trouble is he? Hang on!' and in no time the main gate to the premises is being unbolted and a girl wielding a pitchfork and dressed only in a nightie strides purposefully in my direction.

'Steady on darling!' I protest, holding up my hands, 'There's been a big misunderstanding…'

'A 'gentleman' you said, wasn't it?' she taunts, peering into the half-light. 'I'm not so sure I see one.'

'I ought to have explained myself better, I see that now. I am busy working but have a small errand to do.'

'Oh?'

'It's nothing in particular. Five minutes, no more, but the thing is I –'

'You need someone to keep an eye on your mare?'

'Hallelujah!'

She cocks her head and gradually lowers her weapon, moving closer thus affording us both a better view. Not as old as her voice betrays and naturally fairer of face than her heavily-rouged and distrustful friend, her eyes yet smoulder with a defiant intelligence that equips her well for dealing with general bother such as this. Clearly one not to be trifled with whatever hand she has been dealt, I wonder what she herself gleans in turn as she stares back with curiosity at Belle and I.

'Don't mind Bess,' she says, her tone more even now. 'Her bark is far worse than her bite. These are strange days if ever there were and this ain't no parlour game. We women must be savvy in what we do – and who we do it with.'

'I doubt you not,' I answer, 'and I say again, I apologise if I caused any offence.'

Not acknowledging me, she walks up to the front of the hansom, giving a snort of disdain as she notices my hapless passenger. 'I didn't know I was agreeing to babysit him as well as this priceless beauty.'

'You'd do that?' I ask. 'What do I owe you?', expecting her to name some extortionate fee.

'I don't want your money,' she snaps. 'I'm not your darling, either: I wish only to meet her. I prefer animals to people, and horses best of all, so why don't you go ahead and leave the two of us together?'

In the circumstances this may be the only offer I get and in spite of the girl's gruff manner I instinctively trust her, so rather than risk insulting her again I take my opportunity and hurry to the southern end of the road, bearing left for fifty yards before turning left again into the murk and dinginess of Brooke Street, where all lies in eerie silence.

Home to room upon overcrowded room of wayfaring families or else those engaged in the petty trades, its stances of miserable-looking shops wilt in the permanent shadow of rows of high tenements which loom either side like teetering black icebergs, built here, so they say, in days of yore when the City had its own wall. Enticed on only by the lure of my reckless assignment, I step over sorry piles of cast-out things of no value even to the able scavengers who scour every nook and cranny and who'd sooner hawk their grandmother's teeth than wander empty-handed. A less likely refuge for a scrivener of dreamy verse could never be imagined even by the immortal Poet who once lived and worked here – but after a brief search I locate what I believe to be the fabled door, thrilling to find that at some point in the night a careless inhabitant has left it slightly ajar.

My heart beats in my chest like a tenor drum as I reverently touch the splintered frame, glancing left and right as I push it open, murmuring to myself:

'A humble form the Godhead wore, the pains of Poverty he bore.'

Inside, a dank, narrow passageway leads to a rickety staircase, lit only by a piece of guttering tallow. I creep in, quivering like a timid church mouse, halting after a few steps when I catch the report of an ominous rattling sound. Motionless as I listen yet unable to discern the cause, I tiptoe up to the first floor, nearly laughing aloud in relief as I come across the pitiful sight of an old charwoman sat with her dustpan and brushes, snoring in her rocking chair. Desiring not to rouse her, I sneak on by, still straining to see in the feeble candlelight as I ascend three stories more, passing the doors to several lodgings before I reach the uppermost level.

Pleased to rest for a moment, I find that of the two crude dwellings squeezed into the original roof void one has been boarded-up, signs of a recent blaze a stark reminder of the parlous lives lived by those in such makeshift setups. The second door belongs to the east-facing room, the one that holds my interest. Pressing my ear against the worm-eaten wood, I hear nothing; checking the landings, I know it is now or never so I steel myself and turn the handle, wincing as the hunk of ancient oak creaks loudly open, echoing around the stairwell. Hit by a cloud of moths and the whiff of camphor, I gag and nearly flee; yet no vicious curs or querulous occupants appear from within so I cover my mouth and intrude even further, ducking under lines of dripping clothes strung hopefully between the attic beams.

In the musty air of the one room one-bedded garret flat, the dying embers of a mean coal fire still glow in a rudimentary grate and through the propped-open window of the dormer I can make out scores of chimneys and the great dome of St Paul's rising out of the fog like a lost isle in an ever-shifting sea. A shaft of moonlight pours its cosmic silver onto the dishevelled bunk below: could this really be the very chamber where once he toasted his loaf and tossed his doggerel – and this, the bedstead where he dipped his pen and breathed his bitter last? A scrape behind me breaks into my thoughts. At the door, a woman stands watching, beholding me with something close to fear.

'No-one told me you were coming,' she whispers. 'You are here about the rent, I know it. Please show a little more patience and I'll settle what I owe. Just a day or two more and I'll have it for you.'

'Madam…' I begin.

'It's been a sore few weeks but our crisis here is nearly over and things will surely come aright.'

'Really, miss –'

Her demeanour suddenly brightens.

'All is quiet: no-one is here,' she confides, smiling slyly, removing her shawl and bearing the gnawing cold in the scantiest of corsets.

I inch away.

'Do I not please you?' she questions me, taking hold of my

sleeve and pulling me towards her, so that first I smell the gin and then the milk that rises from her breast.

'I am not here for…I tell you I am not the man…'

She bites her lip and her brow glistens with the germ of a marvellous idea as from behind her, still clinging to her skirt, she pushes forward a wide-eyed child of nine or ten.

'She is young…' she leers.

'Miss!'

'…pretty…'

'No!'

I wrestle free from her clutches and run from the room, tearing blindly down the stairs and barging past the post of the open-mouthed domestic, out through the door and into the night, swaying down the street like some ten-a-penny soak till my head swims, my knees buckle and I sink to the ground, retching into the gutter.

My return sees good old Belle in clover, sung to and mollycoddled and devouring a cupful of sugar lumps, a just reward for all her work.

''Ello!' the woman cries. 'We thought we'd lost you. Thought you'd abandoned her, she did! A whole quarter of an hour you've been!'

'I'm very sorry. I lost all track of time.'

'Don't fret! I'm only having you on. She's been as quiet as a lamb, ain't you pet? We're quite inseparable now. Hey – are you feeling alright?'

'I'm fine,' I tell her. 'I got a bit dizzy, that's all,' adding, as I notice the trap is empty, 'any clue where he's got to?'

'Oh, he's a fly one, him!' she chortles. 'No sooner had you gone when he peels open his eyes and jumps out, sober as a judge. Took off without so much as a 'by-your-leave'… not before he dropped this though.'

She hands me a dainty velvet purse, the only things inside a silver hairpin and a solitary shilling piece. The charge for his journey should be at least double that but as he has only been half a burden I tell her, 'Thank you, but please keep it – no: I insist. Get yourself a warming nip.'

'Nah, I don't touch the stuff no more. Come up in the world since I saw you last.'

I stare back at her blankly. Priding myself on never forgetting a face - such a knack part of a proper cabman's stock-in-trade - I have absolutely no recollection of her. It must be an honest mistake on her part, so I make no fuss and smile as politely as I can, kicking away the chocks and retaking my seat.

'You still don't recognise me, do you?'

Thinking her addled, I anxiously feel for the reins.

'Yes: I know you,' she persists, an errant glint in her eye, 'even if you don't remember me. Broke my heart you did when I was just a silly girl and I am punished for it every day. By the looks of things though we've both come through it for the better and I've learnt to hold no grudge – but I'll be damned before I let another man hurt me. Time heals, but you still have much to answer for, Master Carter.'

'I have changed,' I start, chastened at the mention of my name. 'I am a new man now.'

'You have tamed your wild words, that is true – but what of your wilder ways?'

'I found God and am born again. You can be too.'

'God?' she exclaims. 'I used to kneel and pray but when last I looked the sky was empty.'

'He is up there. Believe me! Try reading Psalm 139.'

'Reading?' she hisses. 'I leave that to you.'

It is all too much so I tug twice and the trap jerks forward.

'Fare thee well, Jeremiah, the 'Weeping Prophet',' she cries. 'A shame you never went and wept over me…'

Belle breaks into a gentle trot and though the woman gives no chase I feel her scornful stare like ballast in my wake, so I chivvy her on, riding away from the wild screams and braying laughter that hang in the air like portents of doom in debauchery's final death throes.

In just a few minutes we are rattling by the gates of the Bailey, the cathedral steps and then onto Cheapside, driving into the heart of the Square Mile as we reach the major crossroads at Threadneedle Street. Behind the sombre grey façade of the Old Lady untold destinies are determined and in the here and now of the pre-dawn drift I must fix my compass too.

The choice laid before me seems plain enough: the road north to the outliers of Hoxton and St Luke's seems futile and unappealing and I will not be tempted west again to duel with these phantoms of another man's life. It is but a hop and a skip to London Bridge and thereafter on to Southwark and the world I hold so dear. I know very well where I long to be and that this is likely my last chance to steer us quietly home…but since Alice's passing I have avoided Bermondsey after dark, fearing that I might return to find her cold and broken form still lying in the hall at Albert Street, whispering my name.

In any case, it feels like a thunderstorm might just be brewing and I am nothing if not a London tradesman to my boots who will go wherever profit leads me. East it is then, to the last exit for the lost – but astray indeed is the sheep who on its arrival there feels joy at reuniting with its flock. For was not Christ more imperilled by an hour spent with the Elders than by forty days alone in the Wilderness? And in our roundabout passage from this life to the next, I have found Man to be never more companionable than when he takes a ride…for in the midst of life we are in death and, in company or not, as we wait to know our fate, all men do ride alone.

8

A Random Fare

Midway along Leadenhall Street and in sight of Aldgate, Belle pulls up, bringing us to a halt. I have not noticed her limping and cannot believe that she is thirsty again but expect I can pinpoint the issue, so I fish around in the bottom of the Gladstone and with a bit of luck lay my hand on the closest thing to a toeing knife. Jumping down, I playfully ask her what her game is, pat her rump and lift up a slightly cracked hoof; beyond the normal wear and tear, though, there is nothing much to see, and I am at something of a loss. Alert also to the growing interest of a band of roughnecks, I do not care to break longer than I need and having spruced her up as best I can we press on east through the Janus-like City.

Indisputable bedrock of our great Christian Empire's commerce she may well be; yet, though I have never left these shores (and probably never will, unless it be as a condemned man) it is hard to conceive of a place of more frightful contrasts, the most lavish dinner parties and ostentatious displays of impossible wealth all too often drawing their Venetian blinds to instances of the direst penury, the admiring passer-by well-advised not to inhale too deeply lest he choke on the crumbling alabaster.

But for our grey imperial paymasters who tally only in pounds and pence it seems that reality has finally come home to roost…as my eyes start to water and my chest tightens I become conscious of a nearby conflagration and discord, evidently the origin of Belle's unrest with her animal fear of fire. Quickly pocketing the borrowed blade and wrapping my cloak around me, I shout a few words of encouragement and coax her forward to investigate the cause.

In front of the entrance to the Underground an angry mob has gathered, waving placards, chanting slogans and holding torches aloft which they keep alive behind a barricade of burning bins. Flying embers engulf the road and small explosions and flashes make the steps look like the descent into Hades, an impression reinforced by the thick, tarry smoke belching like dragon's breath back out of the padlocked gates.

Erected on an unmarked plague pit containing upwards of a thousand bodies, Aldgate station had a difficult start in life and is still shunned by superstitious locals. Today, a new reaper moves among us, in many ways deadlier and more discerning than the consummate killer of two centuries past. His grisly work has hit a raw nerve here, even amongst the long-suffering populace who have long suspected - not without good reason - that their views are ignored and their everyday lives of little concern to the ruling class, their ire now boiling over as the ongoing scandal becomes a touchstone for a litany of loosely-connected causes.

'Irish Home Rule!', 'Women's Rights!' and 'Beware The Star of Judea!' poke out above the melee. The police, of course, are notable only by their absence and as the pall starts to clear more trouble awaits us as we are confronted by a ten-strong East End welcoming committee.

'Who goes there? What is your business here?' a man's voice demands, as a row of red and malevolent faces stare up at me from the asphalt.

'My name is Carter and I am looking for a hire,' I flatly answer, always brought up to give no quarter.

'Then look elsewhere. You seen him here before lads?'

'Not I!'

'Nor me!' another puts in, seemingly sensing blood.

'That is strange,' I counter, 'for I am on the job most nights.'

'What is strange is that you are abroad at such an hour.'

'You too it seems. Yet beggars can't be choosers, can they? Now, if you will kindly let me pass...'

'Not so fast, Dick Turpin! If you really wish to proceed then you must consent to us checking inside your cab.'

'Be my guest,' is my sole reply.

A couple of the men step up and ham-fistedly grope about, much to the irritation of the mare; but armed with no knowledge of the contraption it is like observing children fumbling with a new toy. Confident, so long as they do not notice the bag wedged between my feet, I hum a merry ditty and let them pry.

'Nothing here, boss,' one of them disappointedly reports.

'Just as well. What do you say, Horace?'

'I say that it is an uncommon way to earn a crust…yet a man must be allowed to make his living, after all.'

'Hm. Is that agreed?' he asks. 'Very well,' he relents, '– but be sure to take a good note of his number.'

The rest of the group fall into line and a path is cleared as their leader escorts me on.

'Be our eyes and ears, Carter, cab 2704 – and whatever you do beware the Knife! The Prince of Evil has set his stall on our streets and it will take the vigilance of all honest men to unseat him from his throne.'

I tip my cap and manoeuvre past the ranks of protesters, receiving a few testy barbs and a present of phlegm as I battle to steer Belle safely through the maul. Someone urges me to 'Repent!' and an old man is hauled away yelling, 'He must needs go that the devil drives!' Looking down I notice the dog collar under his hood. His banner reads:

'The Jews are the Men who crucified Christ.'

In open scorn at the people's bravest efforts the heavens now open, the downpour succeeding in dispersing most of the muster faster than the hoot of any crazed assassin. Leaving just a hardy few of the would-be avengers to their watch, we splash on into the night, chopping left and right into the very bowels and entrails of Whitechapel's near-impenetrable warren of rat-infested rookeries, doss houses and blind courts. Passing a succession of low dens and notorious drinking holes, I marvel to see even the likes of The Crown and The Ten Bells all silent or shuttered up, as if in the shared hope that by doing so the worst-laid plans of the primal thing that haunts us might be baffled by our unforeseen abstinence. As ever, though, there are those out there who seem oblivious to it all, one such specimen sloping out of the shadows and staggering out into the narrow lane just twenty yards in front of me…

'Ship ahoy!' I warn her, needing her to move but preparing to slow down.

Turning to see the vehicle bearing down on her, she waves at me expectantly like one who has spotted a trusted friend, failing to budge and compelling me to stop the cab altogether. Unlike the other women I have encountered tonight, this one is far too long in the tooth for these shenanigans and is old enough to be my mother. Haggard, sallow-cheeked and missing her two front gnashers, she has seen her better day, her hefty-looking frame the consequence not of a well-fed stomach but of the need of the dirt-poor citizen to carry their every possession on their person, unable to rely on a roof for the night yet not so naïve as to trust in others in the event that they manage to secure lodgings. Her clothes are old and dirty and the rain that flattens her hair has not been sent to cleanse or baptize her – just as he who stalks and kills her kind has not yet been baptized.

'Come on lady,' I cajole her, 'please get out of my road.'

'It's mine to use as much as it is yours,' she slurs.

'Oh, you're using it alright!' I rag her.

She cackles like a plump witch and takes my insult in good heart but is clearly a danger to herself and others, swaying to and fro in just her stocking feet.

'Ain't you got somewhere to go to?'

'Yeah! I got a half-share of a bed,' she lies, '– soon as I can find the money. What about you? You out long? Where you from?'

'None of your business.'

'Alright! Go easy now! I only wanted a chinwag. It's been like the Mary Celeste round here. Hey – you'll know where's busy. Where shall I go?'

'If it's company you want you'll have better luck down the docks.'

'You'll take me there?'

'No free rides here, I'm afraid.'

'I never said nothing about free, did I? I can pay my way, you cheeky devil,' – in one swift movement sliding her hand into her bodice and proudly pulling out a threepenny bit.

As she flashes her ill-gotten gains I warm to her sauciness and reflect that her lucre is as good as the rest; still, I have no more margin for sentiment tonight and have drained my fund of cab-man's largesse.

'I'm sorry but the charge would be three times that.'

'I do not have it,' she pouts, 'but I will go and get it for you. Wait here, for I shan't be long,' disappearing down the mouth of a forbidding-looking alley before I can reply. Kicking myself, I am now stuck between my calling and my conscience.

As the storm sets in I sit and wait patiently as three, then four, then five minutes go by, with no sign of her return. In the natural way of things, as my grandfather Josiah would have said, she would not even be here, a woman's place being in the home, and it is there that they flourish in their rightful domain just like the olive tree planted in fertile soil...but the world is changing and, of late, have come the clarion calls pushing hard for a new order, one in which women are not just seen but heard and represented, their role no longer set in stone. In my mind I can understand it but my gut tells me that it bodes ill for the future of our race and is it not already the case that our greatest figurehead is an Empress and a Queen – and, what is more, the most highly favoured of all, a low-born handmaiden?

Some of them now demand equality and even votes, seeking to rise up and drive a coach and horses right through the old traditions and long-accepted practices of countless generations. Yet we are boys built on our mother's milk, weaned whilst still tied to her apron strings, anchored like ships in safe harbours and hauled in in the glory of our youth. We know nothing better than her cloying wisdom until one day the painter is cut, and, set elsewhere, a woman's love becomes the torpedo that scuttles our fleet or the jagged reef on which our proudest galleons founder.

It is all part of an unstoppable tide, I think, that will sweep the old society away, and in a sense I am also inclined to agree that there is need for significant change; but I, for one, have my misgivings over what will happen when we put power in the hands of those who are not accustomed to it – and when they are given their freedom see how they use it!

Shivering and cursing the woman for wasting my time, I wonder how much longer I can afford to delay. Just then, I hear voices as two swarthy sorts appear, walking quickly and deep in debate about something, their row cut short the moment they clap eyes on the sight of the resting mare…

'Hulloa! What is this, Isaac?' one of them exclaims.

'It is a gig – and she seems to stand idle!'

'Idle, aye, but not unattended. You sir! Why are you here?'

'I am waiting on a customer,' I say, as casually as I dare.

'Who?'

'A woman.'

'Oh? What is her name?'

'I do not know.'

'Her address, then?'

'She did not tell me.'

He snorts. 'And where exactly were you proposing to take her, this woman, who is not here and who you tell us you do not know?'

'To the river.'

'Indeed! And what then?'

'To…wherever my work takes me.'

'A cock and bull story if ever I heard one,' is the verdict of his acquaintance.

'Most irregular, Jabez. I reckon him to be a crawler. Our lenience has been tested far too long. This is not a cab rank - *sir* - and you have no right to loiter.'

'But my fare…'

'Don't make me laugh.'

'To hell with her!'

'And what then of the Knife?'

'Leave him to us!' he growls. 'We will run him to earth – and God help him when we do, so as you value your life move on!'

He drops a cosh out of his sleeve and I need no further prompt. Unable to turn the cab round in such a tight space we roll forward through a narrow archway. Having got us into this maze my challenge now is to find a way back out.

The task, however, is much easier said than done, as a series of obstructions, diversions, and shambolic new edifices thrown up in record time conspire to create a conundrum to tax the knowledge of even the most time-served jarvey. It is impossible, too, to not be affected by the prevailing mood of dread or the tableaux of tragedy played out in every quarter: vague forms lie senseless in squalid doorways as cripples and dolts take what shelter they can in bulks, the whole scene a jarring cluster of hopelessness, dirt and disease. Those still conscious yell out pleas as the trap rattles by and a ravenous few pick over the same foul scraps as the wheeling, marauding gulls, on their hands and knees but with no esteem for either heaven or hell.

More concerned now with resetting my bearings than lining my pockets, I ignore those most in need of my ministry as I seek a suitable exit, the only clue to my exact whereabouts the brewery clock that somewhere behind me chimes half-past three. It is all to no avail though and it seems the harder I try the more I am caught in a trap of my own devising, close to my wits' end as the weather worsens and the rain bounces off the cobbles.

Hardly seeing or thinking straight anymore, as if by magic a manic figure in a top hat pops up right in front of me. Hopping from one foot to the next in the downpour he dances about like a giant ant on hot coals as he frantically waves his umbrella to flag me down, calling out 'A ride, sir, a ride!' and much as I'd rather plough on and solve my riddle, I slow, then reluctantly stop...

'Mercy me!' he blows, his cuffs and coattails dripping. 'At last: a man in this abysmal city who appreciates some work!'

Considering the where and the when, I have him at a glance and know all too well his type: he is a gentleman slummer, a Mr Moneybags, with his haughty airs and shiny new shoes, here to mix it with the natives for a few sordid hours before fleeing back home to the arms of mammon and the redemption that only currency can buy.

He is one - what with his clean collar, waxed moustache and solid gold fob chain - that any blaggard would lick his lips at the prospect of, prime prey at a country mile, yet he evidently lives a charmed life and is poised to make his escape again tonight with his marbles intact and none the wiser as to the certain downfall he courts.

'Where to, sir?' I ask him, with little alacrity.

'Ach, nowhere in particular,' he sniffs. 'I merely want a ride.'

'East or west then?

'I care not. Show me adventure. Take me where you will.'

'You can pay?'

'Always!' he declares, roaring with abandon.

'Then...what will you give?'

In answer he flicks me a sovereign and climbs into the seat. 'I have another for you too, if need be. For this, though, I would give my very soul.'

I nod. 'Very well. Just as you wish.'

Turning the cab and driving hard into a dense yellow squall, I head east - ever east, for there the sun rises - taking the route of least resistance until I spy a gap between two houses, and, leading us through, happen upon a rare strip of vacant land, the remnants quite possibly of an ancient burgage.

Incongruous amidst the wider rampant grabbing of unclaimed space, this last vestige of greenery will not doubt soon be fair game the moment its tenure elapses. For now, however, its few bushes and patches of foliage are a merciful release from the schemes of men – and, it seems, also home to a pack of stray dogs, who regard the pungent smell of the mare and the sudden appearance of the vehicle as both a menace and an opportunity worthy of investigation. All look in need of a good square meal and although I count myself an animal lover and have real sympathy for their plight it was never our way to keep pets and we knew that even our best-loved horses were in fact our most valuable tools: our smith's anvil, our gravedigger's mattock, our shepherd's crook.

As they stir and make their move I shake the reins and urge Belle on; hampered, though, by the rough terrain, they soon catch us up and start to worry and nip at her heels. Leaning over, I holler a mixture of commands and threats and seek to fend them off with a few wild swings of my crop but they persist undeterred, slavering and snarling and clearly relishing every aspect of the hunt. It is a close-run thing and I fear that the mare might be provoked into doing something rash – to my astonishment, though, she takes matters into her own harness, first yanking us left into what I would have held to be a dead-end courtyard, then sharp right down a suspect-seeming wynd and - lo! - out into the open as I find us back on track and miraculously heading along the Commercial Road East!

I cannot suppress my elation and shower her with praise, giving her her head as a canter turns into something close to a gallop, our rabid tormentors eventually giving up the chase as we clatter past a long parade of faceless warehouses, ill-lit factories and ugly depots. Here, at the forgotten fringes of the city, lies the throbbing engine that powers it all, the coal-black seam from which is hacked the glittering stone. Known only as the 'Abyss' I seldom have call to come here but he has asked for adventure and adventure he will get for I will now not surrender any of my bounty, and as we turn towards Stepney I can no longer distinguish between the peals of thunder and the rumble of our wheels.

We skirt by sidings and ride under the shadow of sprawling chemical plants, dye factories and stinking gas-works, contenders surely to be amongst the most tortuous constructions ever raised by the human hand, passing street upon street of small brick houses, built for the armies of worker bees who toil invisibly day and night at the service of the hive. Looking out toward a spoiled, muddy shoreline and the rotting hulk of a man-o'-war, these people's music is the relentless clank of heavy industry and the distant toot of steam packets coming into dock...yet amidst the desolation and the easy derision of those so quick to judge, it remains true that for most this is a home from home and that the brackish shallows of reclaimed bog will be their only ever Eden.

Better connected with the rhythms of the river and sayings of the sea than the manners of the land, as we near Limehouse Basin we pass a knot of men huddling outside a lime oast. Turning to look, they whistle and make comic catcalls so riling and upsetting my passenger that he gets to his feet and returns their harmless banter with violent aplomb – at which point one of them runs forward and hurls a rock towards us narrowly missing the horse's haunches. Narked by his sheer recklessness, I halt the cab and admonish him and instruct my fare to retake his seat forthwith; in answer, he laughs feverishly and beats against the cab roof with his cane, unrepentant and disinterested in all I have to say, pledging to pay me whatever fee I might require and urging me to carry on.

Biting my tongue, we head down East India Road, its few remaining traditional and specialist shops a reminder of a bygone age when the wharfside echoed to the beat of hammers and the steady strokes of the sawyer's arm. Once a pivot of the seafaring and shipbuilding world, it is now is a ghetto of castaway faces packed like sardines into bare and tiny rooms in private lodging houses, often little better than disused shops. Carrying bedding and prayer rugs with them wherever they go, importing their own food and keeping to distinct and rigid tribes, where they do cohabit the Hindu and the Buddhist tend to eat apart from one another, and both will take great steps to avoid the Mohammedan, though he mostly be quiet and inoffensive and his meal be only one of rice.

One such exile raps impatiently at a numberless door squeezed between a ropemakers and a ships chandlers, admitted inside with extreme prejudice by an elderly Cantonese and his mute dogsbody before the portal is slammed shut and barred from within. I have a good notion of what delightful cures he will find dispensed by those who rule this particular roost, and what bitter contrition he will taste when he finally surfaces on the morrow – or more likely, the morning after; yet all horsemen know of forks in every highway down which some men will venture only once.

Venturing ourselves beyond the Cut, the signs of order and activity grow less frequent and familiar, the one storey blocks giving way to pairs of cottages then lonely hovels and shacks, until we pass the final factory and what I deem the last outposts of civilization. The whole horizon seems to stretch out in front of us and

I have driven as far as anything worth seeing and as far as I am prepared to go. Having strived to give him his money's worth, I ease up, relieving Belle of the strain. If anything, the grey and rutted road to Poplar looks even bleaker when illuminated by a sudden flash of lightning and of no mind in this deluge to observe pointless niceties, I start to swing the cab around – at which point the hatch flies open and my man's head pops up like a jabbering jack-in-the-box.

'Ain't this fun, driver? What a night this is! Ah, sweet remembrance of the sea! Where to next, I wonder?'

'I think we have come quite far enough.'

'We go back west?'

'Yes.'

'And then?'

'Then I take you home.'

'Home?'

'Yes indeed, sir: where is it?'

'Everywhere and nowhere.'

'Come now,' I humour him, growing weary of his antics. 'It is getting late and a few pointers would not go amiss.'

He stays silent.

'I see. Have it your own way then.'

'Oh, don't worry – I will.'

He stands up to his full height on the leather seat, proffers his hand and I hold out mine in return and in one swift movement he snatches the crop and reins from my grip, proceeding to beat at Belle who whinnies in pain and takes off across the pitching, careering like the clappers in the direction of the causeway. In shock, I reach forward and try to wrest control from him but he shakes me off and throws me back with a prodigious strength I would hardly credit him for. Lying winded in my chair, I watch aghast as he flogs the mare without restraint and compels the hansom along the soft clay road, eventually steering us into a narrow strait that leads to a semi-flooded wasteland of abandoned brickfields. I plead with him to desist but he orders me to be quiet for it is now he who has the whip hand, and I slump back in horror

123

as he rides ever on, dragging us further by the furlong from where we ought to be.

He drives madly like a Jehu, my cab his battle chariot, silt and spray flying from its wheels, and as the tempest rages we truly feel the valediction of an English summer.

The sodden ground starts to sink beneath us as a dense bank of sea-fog rolls in, the only bit of light the glow of the sleepless iron-works and scattered smelting bars. Howling hideously, he seems to believe that he can singlehandedly corral the elements, and if he has a new destination in mind its name eludes me as he takes us beyond the geographical limits of human goals and human gods. Praising the night, whipping-up Belle into a frenzy, he screams some fallen angel's death song and my mottled grey transforms before my eyes into a fire-breathing, jet-black Púca. The great river itself has long receded and I can hardly see five yards in front of me yet she runs on wrathfully into oblivion and I dare not make another bid for the reins with her out of her mind and charging at full tilt.

Eventually, with one last terrible ululation, he pulls the vehicle to a sharp brake; with it, the rain ceases and the storm abates as quickly as it came.

'Will this do you, sir?' he turns and leers.

'Enough,' I croak, Belle's quaking body glistening with sweat, her broiling breath condensing in the haar.

'But surely not?' he frowns. 'I hazard we might go a little fur-ther…'

'No!' I plea. 'For the mare's sake.' Then with a wince, I ask him: 'Where are we?'

He raises his eyebrows in mock surprise and leaps down. 'What's this? A London cabbie out his depth?'

'Yes,' I admit. 'I am lost.'

'Let me direct you then. Take a good look. I have brought you to the edge of forever.'

I gaze about me, seeing only a tract of dreary marsh and flatfish that flail in the shallows at his feet, dying in the brown, metallic waters.

'Who are you?'

'Do you really not know?'

He lifts his hat and I look again and the scales fall from my eyes as I see that it is no toff who stands before me but my co-conspirator of the dusty plain.

'Blow me down!' I say. 'Y–yet it cannot be!' disbelieving of the evidence before my eyes not just due to his fancy new raiment but, more still, the ripe anger in his face.

He weighs my reaction, then slowly nods. 'Yes,' he whispers. 'It is I.'

'My old comrade,' I manage to recover, 'what a lucky day! What chance has brought you here?'

'You.'

'Me?' I baulk, paralysed with fear.

'I am glad that you remember me for I presumed you had forgotten. Hard have I hunted you and many a fare have I wasted in tracking you down. I waited patiently for the souls you promised to send me – yet how many ever come? I do not take well to treachery and you must know that in the place where I dwell a week is more like an eternity.'

'I confess that you have slipped my mind of late,' I tell him. 'I have had much to deal with and not a few distractions but I will try to do better, forsooth.'

'A man's promise is easily broken.'

'You will give me more time though, surely?'

'For now. But I will not come looking for you again…and I never ask twice.'

He moves closer and tosses the crop back to me then tells me to hold out my hand. As I do, he reaches up and pays me another gold coin, closing my fingers into my clammy palm.

As I try to pull away another wave of freezing fog sweeps in, invading us like an eleventh pestilence. His grip loosens as the vapour encircles him and all that can be heard is the sharp hiss of steam and the faraway cry of some stranded ocean bird. I shut my eyes and cover my mouth as I wait for it to clear, and as the wind that carries it in brings with it fresh news of lawless lands I ask if

126

I can somehow summon the courage to state my faith – or even to openly defy him. Martyrdom may be the one thing he is not ready for and who is to say even he cannot be plucked from the depths?

In answer, an icy blast cold enough to stir the dead tells me that I can delay no more. If I leave him here - even at his own behest - I flout a cabman's most basic duty, and with that all that my sires ever taught me. No: I can and will not, and must be that good shepherd – so long as he allows me. I pick a psalm at random - 'You, Lord, are a shield around me, my glory, the One who lifts my head high,' - that perhaps we can recite together, and, sensing that the murk must have at least partly dispersed, open my eyes to embrace him…but all that remains is a grey mare and her master, and under the raw and boundless beauty of a newly-spangled sky my passenger-cum-coachman has gone.

9

Pearly Kings and Pearly Queens

Before I can consider going anywhere or think about what to do next I must first attend to Belle. Her ordeal over, it looks like she is utterly done for, signalling the end to our night; but, exhausted as she is, the indisputable fact remains that we are miles away from home and must stick together more than ever before if we have aspirations to see the morning sun.

With nothing for her nosebag, I pull my tried and trusted trick of singing her a gentle lullaby – for once, though, she does not so much as turn her head and the thought occurs to me that she cannot possibly know that the blows that rained down on her did not issue from my hand. Unable to bear the notion and not wanting to further pressure her or even shake the reins, the only way to break the deadlock is to climb down and seek to walk by her side. This she readily takes to, vigorously rubbing her muzzle against my lead arm, and as the cloud disappears I glimpse the twinkling lights of Cassiopeia seeming to beckon us thither. Standing next to her reminds me of our first outing together, with I more pony boy than cavalry man, and as the laddish love I first felt for her comes flooding back I call to mind a different horsey ballad that might just fit whilst doing my best not to betray my own doubts and fears...

> *'A mare who came*
> *without a name*
> *into my shadow's silence,*
> *And there her same*
> *and sacred flame*
> *put paid to night's shrill violence,*

From moor and wold
and dawn's sweet cold
to city's blackest furnace,
Her gilded mane
was first to tame
as twilight's boldest Witness...'

...and *that*, please let me tell you, is not from the pen of the Bard nor one of the guiding Fathers, but Carter, J., native of Bermondsey.

Paddling along a flat and featureless foreshore, I gaze upward for information...

'It's a braw bricht moonlit nicht. How much do you know about the Universe, Jeremiah?' a voice from the past inquires.

I sense his bent and aged form. 'About as much or as little as any Christian can, I guess.'

'No: I mean the galaxies, the solar system, the massed constellations.'

'I used to know a lot as a boy. You showed me so much...but most of that's been forgotten long ago.'

'You should take it up again. There's no time and place like a clear night on Earth for making a sketch of Heaven.'

'Funny. I always saw it as a kind of Hell: a void of eternity, the dull and hopeless cold.'

'Perhaps it depends on where you look. Still: show me what you can remember.'

I start with the simple ones.

129

'The easiest cluster,' I offer, 'is the Great Bear. Firstly, you need to find the Plough. As the equinox approaches, in a northern sky, the Plough is tilted on its side so that it looks more like a man about to dive into deep waters. But the Plough is just the lead pattern and the Bear itself is made up of several other stars.'

'Good.'

'Next, I suppose, is the Little Bear. It's like a dimmer, distorted version of its older brother but it's important for the presence of Polaris, the Pole Star, used by sailors, you once told me, as a helpful guide when navigation was a hit-or-miss affair. Right now, the best way I can describe it is like a spade that's digging earth.'

'Excellent Jeremiah!' he encourages me. 'Anything else?'

'The other obvious one at this time of year is Cygnus, the Swan, one of the most spellbinding constellations in the sky. Some folk refer to it as the Northern Cross but to me it's a blatant cruciform.'

'What's the difference?'

'Everything in the world, father.'

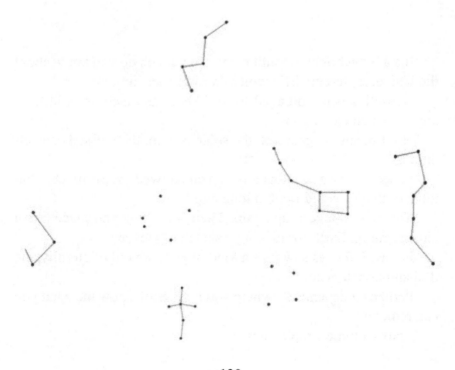

'You have learned as much? Bravo! And what about that misty spot over there: the one between Pegasus and Cassiopeia?'

I rack my brains. 'Hang on a minute: it's on the tip of my tongue…it's…it's…Andromeda.'

'Yes! Andromeda, the great spiral: the most distant thing visible to the naked eye. The rays of light reaching us from her stars set out an eternity ago – when our ancestors still dragged their knuckles in the clay. What we're witnessing - right here, right now - are the ailing rumours of things that really did happen but in an era so far-flung and so remote that Andromeda herself has long forgotten them: in other words, the truth and a fairy-story being told to us at the same time.'

'And what about our strange visitor?' I ask.

'You mean him?' he gestures with his chin towards a barely-visible fantail of light with a mixture of reverence and fear. 'The least said the better.'

I chuckle.

'Laugh not! He is ever a bringer of woe. Tonight, his fire burns a trail in the west…'

I thrill at the remembrance and Belle snorts her approval, her morale picking up as she finds herself unencumbered by ungrateful human cargo. Clearer now in where I ought to head for, we kick-on across the mire but for well over a mile I see precious little sign of progress; then, at last, I snatch a fleeting glimpse of a yardarm and geeing her on to make one final heroic push we find ourselves on a section of hard standing that leads us to the periphery of The Highway. After my close brush with oblivion never have the middens of Limehouse seemed so picturesque and endearing – and never before in my life have I felt so grateful to be back within the sound of Bow bells!

Devoid - for but a few hours - of the full-throated appeals of its bands of coolies and costers, in the creeping mist and patchy gaslight it almost possesses an air of unrequited romance. Here are T. J. Skinner & Sons, the pelters, and there is Murphy's, the knackers, where my well-meaning father once dragged me out into the stinking yard on a boiling July day and made me…but never mind that.

We pass a Baptist Church then a Wesleyan Day School, a Methodist Chapel and a Friends Meeting Place, and much as I would never contest that the Latter Day Saints Halls and Presbyterian Alms Houses do anything but worthy, vital works, is it not this very splintering and disintegration of the Holy Writ that opens the door to the One who aims to divide and rule and ultimately vanquish us all? In our vanity, or delusion, as we sought pious perfection, we lost sight of the real prize and became blind to truth, losing ourselves in the process as we pored and bickered over the meaning of every trite pronouncement. To those we aspire to preach and set an example to, all of this is but another unneeded nail in the coffin of their personal reunion with God, a blunt caltrop in the side of every mounted Crusader...yet, here, in the thick of it all, stands the rock of St George-in-the-East – an immovable object, its doors ever left wide open in the lee of such unseemly squabbling.

Dropping down towards the river, we walk right by a former drapers, the scene of the second of the two appalling slayings of just a generation ago. Could it be our modern way of life and the unrelenting push of industry that breeds the wanton slaughter? And are we, by nature or design, no higher really than animals, preordained to strike out and create carnal order of our own as Man is turned into automaton, a shell without a soul, stripped of all dignity, grace and purpose, a state that can only lead to all-out war?

Yet it would be unfair to ascribe these problems solely to London – or even the East End. Yes: horrors have happened here but have they not in every country and just how long could each community's harmony be sustained if, even for an hour, we could lift the rooftops or remove the whitewashed frontages and take a peek inside? And, what then further, if we could do the same with all the people that we meet and know – could we really live with the true knowledge of the misdeeds and grasping schemes that brood behind the kindest or most innocuous of eyes? For do not all of us at certain times wear a mask; some, more than one even if we do not know it, to keep a light from shining too brightly into our own corruptible hearts?

Ah! Here is Mother Thames, and with her hope rises anew, for on her banks I can never be lost. The London Docks and those of St Katharine know no respite, and as we near the first it seems as if our arrival has coincided with the debarkation of a large merchant ship. Lines of corn runners, coal porters and longshore men queue on the landing stages for work as sailors from legion nations run down the gangplanks eager to explore, pray and sup. A vessel of this size's arrival might even make a ripple in the *Lloyd's List* and on the waterfront at such times it is well-understood that all seafaring men are equal, and to offer a smoke or a friendly welcome is to bank on receiving it in return at some faraway or exotic port.

I cannot recall seeing the old harbour so choked with traffic and from our vantage point on the quay I can make out scores of clippers, tugs and haulers, barges, brigantines and even a row of ethnic wooden sailing boats: junks, gaffers, coracles and - still tied fast to their mothership - a pair of pearling dhows. From one of these craft an excitable group of seamen raise a ladder and fix it to a stanchion, whooping and cheering as one by one they leave the mooring and set foot back on dry land. Seeing the wharfside awash with similar throngs, the Arabian crew lay down their things, roll out a carpet and set out cushions to create a kind of Bedouin camp, as a windbreak assembled and a wire grate quickly lit shows that they are no newcomers to the Western dawn.

Kneeling, pointing skywards and giving thanks for their safe passage, they break their fast with a meal of dates and tea, the eldest amongst them noticing me watching and soon beckoning me over as he mumbles something to his heavily-swathed companion. Addressing me in his broken pidgin, I catch the odd word but try as we might we struggle to make ourselves understood until his shipmate intervenes.

'He says that you have a beautiful horse and would very much like to buy her.'

Caught on the hop, I am taken aback more by the lilting voice than by the proposition, belonging as it does to a European woman, who at her captain's behest unfurls her headscarf. Spare and pale, but calm and queenly, I stare at this young adventuress and wonder at her history, a lone white face seemingly willingly in cahoots with these Bahraini boatmen.

'Tell him 'thank you',' I say, 'and that I am grateful for his offer – but she is not for sale at any price.'

On learning of my reply the man shows little emotion and gestures for me to sit by him. Passing me a dish of dried fruit and a cup of the char, he confers with the woman.

'He says that your mare is old but well looked after, not like a London horse. He says that she has something of the desert in her.'

'I know nothing about that.'

'Nonetheless, he is insistent. It is all there in the neck, the poll, the *jibbah*.'

'And I say that she still pulls three hundredweight with ease.'

There is a first hint of a smile but she makes no attempt to translate again before his next edict. 'One moment…he asks if your horse will take anything?'

'She may. What is it that he offers?'

At this the cook steps forward with a cauldron of mush, inside of which he has been steeping some variety of grass. I look at the green slop with some distaste but to my surprise Belle takes to it at once, and as she slakes her thirst I nod my appreciation as the skipper puts aside his food and starts to wax at length, all recounted by the woman.

'In his homeland they tell the tale of the Prophet and his horses. One day, after a long trek across the dunes in the high sun, they came to an oasis and the mounts were set free to run to the fresh water. On the command of The Beloved to stop and return to him, only five obeyed and came back. It was these, it is said, that the Prophet chose to perpetuate their line having passed this test of loyalty and courage.'

'A caring master would surely let his horse go?'

'He says that what we hanker for is not always good for us. Those who drink too quickly sometimes scorch in the heat.'

I politely nod and take a sip of tea, as his entourage look on.

'Permit me, then, to tell him a story in return. The favourite mount of the Emperor Caligula was named Incitatus. The Roman loved his horse better than all other things. He gave him a private stable, fed him oats mixed with gold and covered him with purple blankets. Eighteen slaves attended daily to his every need and he even planned to make Incitatus a consul. But Caligula's reign only lasted four years. He was murdered by his own men and no mention is made of what happened to his fine white stallion.'

'And the moral of your story is?'

'Let horse be horse and god be god. Only fools try to turn ivory idols out of clay.'

Having interpreted my words she waits in vain for an answer as my story makes its impression, her captain now seemingly finished with conversation and distracted by a game of marbles – or pearls.

'He once bred horses then?' I eventually ask, in a bid to the break the silence, feeling I may have offended him.

'He did – before his family learned that there were greater riches to be made from the sea. Now everyone in his village is a pearler, forever out on the water. He was the youngest of seven brothers - all dead now, apart from him - but he says that men will stop at nothing to get the thing they most covet: money…a woman…the perfect pearl. Until you look you never know what you will find inside a hard and blackened shell.'

In demonstration of her point, she loosens her stole to reveal a simple necklace of startling white gems.

'Come hither – he will not mind. Now see. Can you tell the difference between a fake and precious stone?'

I examine the piece and compare the trinkets, their soft sheen and creamy lustre, but having no notion of their worth or a pedigree of picking them, I smile and shake my head.

'I thought not. Yet your eyes are no weaker than mine. It is the same as when you look at a steed. We see what we already know.'

Piqued anew by the scene, her fisher king exercises his voice again through hers.

'He says that it is not easy for a man to find his true vocation. Some never do; others only by chance. He will never forget the first time he took to the waves: a craft of sixty souls, with provisions for four months. A sympathy is quickly born of shared hard-

135

ship, the daily grind of life at sea. Then, after weeks at sail, comes that moment – the maiden plunge into the reef, a rope around your neck, a rock tied to your feet, the rush of the surf flooding your ears. Panic grips you, as you fight to fend off your darkest fears, your fate in the hands of your sahib. Then, bound by duty, you set to your task: just you, a basket and the ocean, dread and self-doubt giving way to acceptance as you and the water become one.' She lowers her voice. 'Deep down in the salty realm, how does the creature born with lungs possibly survive?'

I stare at her quizzically. 'Why, by holding his breath of course.'

'You would think so. That is one way. But a wiser man teaches himself to live without air. Just like a pearler, *you* are endlessly hunting something; let us call it a jewel you have lost. I see it in your face. You seek but you do not find – yet here you still are. You have taught yourself to live without air.'

'You see a lot, miss, I give you that. It is true I no longer have what was once most dear to me. My wife –'

'No. Not her. Something else.'

I stiffen, clutching at her arm, as if the wind has been knocked out of me, before somehow rallying to respond. 'What you speak of,' I gasp, 'can never be found.'

'Then you must move on and act as others do. You must abandon your search and take the next best thing.'

Her skipper, grown suspicious, gets to his feet.

'In two minutes,' she loudly resumes, returning to script, 'you have done all that you can, lifting off the noose, tugging twice, as kicking to the light you pop up like a cork, heaved onto deck like a wriggling record catch.'

'And what then?' I ask.

'Then the fun starts as the crop is laid out! You know you have a good one when she does not yield to the novice hand or give up her prize so easily; the rest can be cut open at your leisure and, once eaten, tossed aside.'

'I see. So his 'vocation' is to be a seller of sea charms?'

'He prefers to call himself a salvager of secrets, a dredger of dreams. What others choose to call him is not his business – nor his concern. He says that on the day he found his first pearl he knew that we were not alone.'

I acquiesce, making sure this time I acknowledge him, putting my hands together and bowing my thanks.

'Listen, then,' she urges, 'to what your heart tells you. Only if you do so can the world once more be your oyster…'

Beside me Belle stamps a hoof and flexes her withers, a sure signal she is ready to go, her remarkable revival reigniting my belief that in tandem we can find a way home. Bidding a last good-bye to the dhow's crew, I turn my attention back to the wharf.

For as far as the eye can see the length of the jetty is now a vibrant hub of humanity, and as we pick our way between the pitches and ingeniously-erected stands, sailors hawk everything from pots and pans to silk and spices, and even winged pets from a small aviary of finches, the whole resembling a mini Turkish souk so that I ask myself if I am really still in England, Con-stantinople – or Xanadu? Once again my grey garners more atten-tion than I would like, leaving me with the impression that half the pre-daylight bazaar would be mine if only I let six feet dwindle to two. Yet beyond the clamour, the beat of the drums and hum of a harmonium, I have the unshakeable sense that the hansom is being followed.

Moving away from the main pier I stop and feign to look in the window of a taxidermist. Of all of God's improbable creations staring back at me with their dusty glass eyes, by far the oddest are the duo I spot in the reflection: two tall, big-boned, strapping wenches, dressed up to the nines and hiding behind their fans, loudly arrayed with knickknacks (perhaps the Bahraini's cheaper pearls?) and, though it is not my place to cast aspersions, a fast and loose idea of fashion and allure – for they can be nothing but a pair of nightwalkers still on the make who have worryingly latched onto us.

I gee Belle on, keeping tabs on them from the corner of my eye, only too conscious that we are two tempting and tasty-looking fish swimming amongst the sharks and sailor-town harpies of Shad-well. No dainty ladies of the night are these who force their way

137

through the hordes like a convoy of Russian icebreakers, yet it is horses for courses and I guess they would not be here if they were not somebody's cup of tea, my sole aim now to shake them off like barnacles scraped from a hull before they have the chance to accost or importune me.

I am spared the trouble, however, as a terrible shindy bursts the bubble of the waterfront: a petrified lass shrieks for help as a gang of navvies attempt to drag her on board their waiting tug, sparking an outraged reaction and the harsh blast of police whistles as the sinister duo who have been quietly dogging me toss away their accoutrements and give immediate chase, revealing themselves not as a couple of feckless Unfortunates but two of H-Division's finest, heavy moustaches and ready truncheons to boot. Never before have I seen woman transform into man, but my amazement is soon replaced by an instinct to bolt with the realization that I myself have been under surveillance; jumping back into the driver's seat and imploring Belle to move, I depart the scene via the Wapping Wall, not pausing until we are at Execution Dock and level, across the Thames, with the dim outline of Rotherhithe.

In the distance west I can just make out the wooden platforms and gaunt steelwork of the much-needed span under construction opposite the Tower, meaning London Bridge itself is still the nearest crossing point – the best part of two miles away. The Thames Tunnel, of course, is not able to accept horses and even the dependable lightermen have vacated their posts leaving me in a serious quandary, for much as Belle has now picked up, in her current state that may as well be the ends of the Earth. As my new-found optimism fades, I suddenly catch the low chug of an engine and turn to see the prow of a barge emerging from the mist. Steering it into its berth, the pilot cuts its power and steps out onto the wharf, securing it to a mooring. Yawning and stretching then sitting on a bollard, he lights a pipe, his attention slowly shifting ashore as he weighs up his next move. Sensing my chance has come, I call to him across the chilly quay.

'Hulloa, sir! I was wondering if you would be able to assist me?'

'No,' he growls, briefly casting me a contemptuous look, then turning his back on me and puffing away.

'My mare and I find ourselves in a bit of a pickle –'

'I am sorry for you, but I am done.'

Having countless times myself been called upon at the end of a long stint, I know exactly how he feels. His point-blank refusal to listen, though, appears to me to be somewhat mean-spirited, so I see fit to remind him of his obligations.

'You have a duty to serve one who sorely needs it.'

'I answer to no man.'

'I doubt your venerable Company would say so.'

'Then go ahead and report me.'

'I have no wish to. Let me make it worth your while instead.'

'Sir – please desist for there is naught you can say that will make me unhitch this rope.'

'I see. So a sovereign would not suit you?'

He exhales deeply. 'It would suit me very well – but where would *you* find such as that?'

'Only right here in my purse.'

I hold it up as proof and when he spies the glint of gold he is a new and different prospect, for I have learnt much in my time as a cabman, above all being the simple truth that every man has his price.

'I am in the wrong employment, clearly then. What do you want?'

'To cross the Rubicon. Nothing more, nothing less.'

'And that is all?'

'Yes. If you can take my horse and trap too.'

'Two souls are no riskier than one.'

Returning to deck, he lowers a side-ramp and even assists in guiding the hansom over the gunwale, and much as it pains me when he collects the tithe and I know I am being held to ransom, the other coin in my possession still means I have had an exceptional night and there is nothing I would not do or pay for the relief and comfort of my grey. That said, the mare is visibly unsure of her new billets, so that I am actually glad for the ever-encroaching haar that masks our true situation. A rare pea-souper, this, and I doubt that even the hoary old port has often seen the likes, and as the ferryman resurrects the vessel's fire-box then casts off without a further word he does well to avoid an early oarsman struggling under the weight of his many eel traps, the heavy reek now aggravated into a solid wall of smog by the fumes of a passing collier, so that the shoreline and then the great river herself are completely swallowed by the brume.

Rather than attempt to cut straight across the water which would be suicide in this murk, he instead brings us round in a long, slow sweep and though the crossing here is barely three hundred yards wide it seems to take forever for the boat to make its trip. I do not make a good passenger, trying to keep my sea legs by fixing my gaze on the sporadic orange glow of his pipe, my deliverance finally coming with a sudden jolt and the crunch of gravel as our escort invites us to take our leave by pointing the way with a bandaged hand.

Here, on the dormant landing stage, scattered figures bearing candles flit about like fireflies but compared to the bustle of the north shore the south bank at St Saviours is like the dark side of the moon. This is where, in 1620, Christopher Jones anchored his ship, had a skinful then set sail with the Pilgrim Fathers aboard the *Mayflower* with a half-baked idea to establish the land of the free – and Belle and I soon pass the inn of the same name, sitting all in darkness. The ship's malnourished crew must have thought that they too had landed on another planet, and in this gloom the only light I can see is a faint yellow pool spilling out from under the door of a nearby building. I step towards it but there is no need for further inspection as I find that Fate has inveigled me back into the company of a once much-loved but lately much-neglected friend – the entrance of The Lettered Board.

Far removed from those mystical winter nights that saw a broken man's faith restored anew, its dirty-white exterior could not stand in starker contrast with those new-fangled bars above the bridges, yet even as I look a steady trickle of men of various types - many dressed for a day's work - quietly greet each other as they meet and cross its threshold.

By any standard it's a disgraceful hour for a person to be in their cups, but taken by a strong desire to step inside my old confessional I hook the hansom to an iron hoop projecting from the wall, tell Belle that I won't be long, and, joining the queue, remove my hat and slip inside under the timber lintel like a salmon drawn back to its spawning grounds, perhaps also to fulfil my own ultimate purpose – or else learn of my final, onerous penance.

10

The Men That Will Not Be Blamed For Nothing

Beer has been brewed from the waters of the Thames for nearly as long as humans have clustered along its banks. The Romans, on conquering these shores, had little difficulty in finding those suitably versed in the uses of meadowsweet and mugwort, and the Norsemen who succeeded them, followed by the French, only added to this knowledge with their deep attachment to forms of mead, wine and bjórr. At the peak of its consumption many hundreds of breweries drew directly from the apparently inexhaustible watercourse, making the site of old Londinium the European capital of the brewer's sacred art, providing fuel for our invaders and nourishment for our own people in the form of the cheap ale taken religiously with every meal, as essential as our daily bread.

In time, alehouses emerged from what had once been a purely domestic tradition with the new role of ale-conner treated quite as seriously as that of Sheriff or abbot. Old methods persisted with landlords creating as well as selling their own special drafts, either ale or beer but never both, for 'ale for an Englysshe man is a natural drinke, must be fresshe and clear, not ropy or smoky, nor it must have no wefte nor tayle.'

Industry's rise changed everything as the bigger breweries soon developed ways of producing large quantities of beer which could be drunk immediately without the expert stewardship of publican or dealer, resulting in a darker, stronger style of beer known after the porters who enthusiastically drank it - and, no doubt, many a hard-working carter too - keeping them going on the hotter days and numbing them in the colder evenings as they braced themselves to do it all over again. Once poured from the jug by barmaids, beer now flowed like manna from mechanical pumps as the men who made it earned vast fortunes serving a need that they themselves had created. Indeed, almost without notice our love and use of beer subtly but forever changed: originally a fillip and in more straitened times a substitute for a proper meal, the nightly knock-me-down turned into the working man's crutch, filling a God-shaped hole in the lives of too many, the only debate being over whether our new-found dependence on its powers of absolution was merely the symptom or the cause.

It was around this time that old Josiah Carter decided he had seen enough, quietly pouring away his stout and eschewing all alcohol, pledging also to never let another drop enter his household – quite a commitment in a thirsty city whose water supply had by common consent long become undrinkable. For the groomsman had begun to despair of the daily spectacle of life's victims tumbling out of the beer shops into the busy streets, and though Christ himself had once turned water into wine, he refused to depart this world with the taste of grapes on his lips, so for Josiah a new plague had been sent to punish the Earth and the new demon was the demon drink.

He was not alone with many sharing his revulsion and concern, as committees were formed, inquiries undertaken, newspaper editors turning over generous column inches to well-known philanthropists and leading social reformers who rushed to preach over the predicament and pain of those only known to the reading pubic as 'the Poor'. Ministers upped the ante, panicked at the drop in church attendances (and, more pertinently, the weekly collection); police and politicians looked in vain to each other, whispering of a return to mob rule. Never before had a pastime stoked such consternation, and even a monarch was moved to lecture her subjects, happily bolstered in her duty by her favourite suppertime toddy.

As such, I know well that Josiah would birl in his grave if he could see me entering this establishment...but there are things a man cannot fully explain even to his own grandfather, and that a parent cannot understand of his own progeny though he try to listen to his words. So much beer has been spilled over this inn's flagstone floor that it can survive a flagon more, and I would fib if I did not admit that my nostrils flared in anticipation of the smell of sweat and damp sawdust, of roasted malt and hops, like the doe that scents for the first bite. Instead, I am hit by the pong of incense, an odour laden with a Pandora's box of associations from a land far, far away. Quite enough to make me heave, I look to make a hasty retreat but my only exit is many others' entrance and as the Rotherhithe faithful flock together in their droves, I realize that if I cannot beat them then I shall just have to join them, jostled forward to be greeted by an usher and directed to one of the last free spaces in the wholly transformed pub's rough-and-ready arrangement of jam-packed and seemingly sober pews.

*

In the few moments I have to freely gaze about, I confirm that I have not disremembered my recent past and have indeed returned to the self-same site of my life and soul's salvation. Practically unrecognizable from the deserted night cellar of those intense winter meetings, due more perhaps to the congregation of new faces than the fabrics or the furnishings, I still see the same scuffed mahogany-topped bar now draped with fine, hand-sewn banners exhibiting some vaguely familiar symbol; and there, too, hanging from the ships mast beams are the row of pewter tankards, today stuffed with lavender and cloves as if their proper purpose is no longer needed or has lately been forgotten. Three large beer barrels have been arranged next to the lit fire to form some kind of raised dais – beyond that, it is impossible to investigate further such is the size and spread of the gathering, all that is visible outside between the windows and the water the shape of a hangman's noose, a warning so familiar to its onetime clientele of deserters, smugglers and crooks.

It is, it seems, a men-only affair, the fairer sex unrepresented within these walls, by chance or intention, I do not know. An incongruent mix pack the tavern in their stead: merchant seamen stand whispering at the unstocked bar joined by hod carriers identifiable from their stoops, whilst on the front row are what look like scholars or churchmen with their robes, flowing beards, and severe deportment. To my left, an old timer fidgets nervously about, whilst to my right a blotchy youth barely out of short trousers - a cabin boy or an indentured apprentice - hovers on the edge of his wooden perch, clearly electrified by the prospect of the advertised proceedings. Verily, these do not look like men who keep thieves' hours and the whole place buzzes with the kind of raw excitement only reserved for a Bank Holiday cock-fight and I never knew of such shared suspense - or hope - in a South London church.

As the taproom door is finally bolted-to somebody somewhere strikes up a beat on a bodhrán, two more quickly picking up a tune on a flute and tin whistle, bringing a sudden respectful hush to the room and heralding the emergence from the pub's snug of a nightmarish half-human, half-bestial procession. Four figures enter, stepping forward in formal line, grotesque in aspect and either bewildering or comical depending on the bent of the uninitiated witness. Each resting a hand upon the figure in front's left shoulder, all but the first are blindfolded: a man in a white cassock who swings a censer and wears an animal mask topped with a stag's skull. Behind him walks a lantern-jawed adherent dressed more plainly bar the fresh stains of flagellation across his midriff, similarly for the last, whilst third in line steps a loosely-shackled soul, clad in a hair shirt and skins yet crowned with a circle of holly that holds in place a long, sweeping mane as he teeters along on fake ungulate hoofs.

Alarmed, I get up but am thrust back down by a wiry arm, the sinewy limb somehow familiar by the inking on its wrist - a bird carrying a flaming sword in its beak - which I now connect to the new banners over the bar and the memory of an unpleasant experience from earlier on in the night. Looking up, I see the face of the vagrant ex-sailor whose cronies very nearly buttonholed me at Blackfriars Bridge.

'Well well, guv'nor,' he rasps, 'fancy meeting you again. I never seen you here before so let me bid you 'welcome' and give you a copy of this.'

'What is it?' I ask him sharply, not well-disposed to my aspiring attacker and wary of any gift he may wish to bestow.

'Now now. It is only the Book of Revelations. It will help you to follow the service here.'

'I need it not for I always carry a copy with me.'

'Not like this one you don't...'

He thrusts it at me and to keep the peace I reluctantly take it, liking it even less so when I look at the volume's cover:

THE BOOK

Of

ꟻƎVƎⱯⱢꞀOИꙄ

'What on earth −?' I frown, but he cuts me off with a yellow finger raised to his cracked lips.

Beside the fire the procession slows to a halt and at its head the figure who I hesitate to call priest holds high his cross and turns to address the room.

'Dearly Beloved,' he begins, his voice partly muffled by his mask, 'we gather here today, as we always do, to offer our thanks and to give praise to the one true Lord. Amongst us I am pleased to find a few new faces, telling me that our ministry is not in vain and that word continues to spread of the work we do along with tidings of the good news. Good news? Doesn't that seem like something we would all welcome? For all we hear of nowadays -

yes, even you, the faithful - is of life's miseries, its chaos and the heinous sin rife amongst our once proud and virtuous people. Indeed, on my way here a street preacher ran to warn me that the end of the world is nigh – and in truth who can blame him for thinking himself not in England but in Gomorrah or in Sodom?'

At this, the first murmur of concord ripples around the bar.

'In the New Testament, Jesus tells us to beware of false idols; to ever guard ourselves against temptation and the empty words of the Pharisees. They sit, he says, upon Moses' seat – but do not do as they do, for they do not practice what they teach. They tie up heavy burdens, hard to bear, and lay them on the shoulders of others. They do all their deeds only to be seen by others. They love to have the place of honour at the banquets and the best seats at the synagogue and to be greeted with respect. They love to have people call them rabbi – but you are not to be called rabbi, for you have one teacher, and you are all students. And, what is more, call no-one your father here on Earth, for you have only one Father – the one in Heaven.'

Confidence grows as the assembly warms to the theme, folk bellowing out a few spontaneous 'Amens!', the speaker now climbing atop one of the beer kegs as his diatribe unfolds.

'But woe betide you, scribes and Pharisees, for you lock people out of Heaven. For though you do not go in yourselves, when others do you stop them. You cross sea and land to make a single convert – and you make the new convert twice as much a child of Hell as even yourselves! Woe to you, blind guides, who swear by the gold of the sanctuary not the sanctuary that made the gold sacred. Woe to you, hypocrites, who clean the outside of the cup and bowl when the inside is full of all kinds of filth. Woe to you, who build the tombs of prophets and the righteous and say, 'If we had lived in the days of our ancestors then we would not have shed their blood'. In saying so you testify that you are descendants of those who murdered all those prophets!' Therefore, I send you prophets and sages who you may kill so that upon you may come all the righteous blood shed on God's good earth…'

Loud applause breaks out, a homage in common, but he signals to all to keep their heads, his sermon now nearing its crescendo.

'Not far from here are buildings masquerading as houses inside of which are hidden places of worship – but not of the Christian kind. Their stated purpose is to offer shelter and sanctuary to those who wish to practice their beliefs. But their real motive is lust, corruption and greed. Your government knows this but is more interested in clinging onto its colonies than protecting its own people. Yet we do not always need the evidence of our senses to know that our enemies are already upon us and growing in number, like the slow rising of a flood: those who would happily profit from our land yet never embrace our faith. It is upon them - and those who bargain with them - that the hardest blow should fall. I do not wish to repeat their name. We know very well who are the men that will not be blamed for nothing.'

In what feels like an unstoppable eruption of emotion the room finally rises as one, giving vent to a pent-up roar of fury like a dam whose walls have finally burst. Unmoved, the stag-priest turns his attention to the prisoner, as one of his acolytes removes his fetters and leads him to a spot much closer to the fire.

'Who caught the first horse?' he asks him.

'It was Cain,' the man answers.

'And where did he catch him?'

'At the east edge of the Garden of Eden, in the way of the Land of Nod.'

'Yes. Cain it was! And because of his daring we have held dominion over beasts ever since…but around before Adam, was I.'

He has full command over the room again.

'It is but one chance we have to reconcile ourselves with God – like the stag that covers hind in the autumn and not again for another year. So help me Lord, in your wisdom, to always keep your secrets and obey your Commandments. If I break any of them I wish no less than my heart be torn from my breast by two wild horses and my body quartered and swung from chains and the wild birds of the air left to pick my bones. And these, then taken down, buried in the sands, where the tide ebbs and flows twice every twenty-four hours to show all who knew me and will ever hear of me that I was a deceiver of the faith.'

149

Holding up a copy of the same book given to me, he beseeches, 'Repeat after me...'

And so follows what I believe to be an invocation, and if it be in English then it is unlike any English I ever heard or read...

"Last the and first the am I. Afraid be don't!',
said and me on hand right his placed he.
One living the am I!
Ever and ever for alive am I now
but, dead was I.'

As I struggle to follow the text he reaches over and picks up something from the mantel...

'Scroll the open and seals the break
to worthy is who?
Fallen have you far how think!'

Forced to kneel, the captive's sackcloth is torn open at the back and a poker pulled out of the flames...

'Throne the before standing, alike small and great.'

Held aloft for all to see, the brand glows white-hot...

'Lords of Lord and kings of King...'

And comes a high-pitched, agonised howl and the sizzle of burning flesh.

The attendants help to lift the man shakily to his feet as the priest collects a plate and Quaich. Muttering a prayer, he commences the Eucharist.

'At the Last Supper, Christ took the bread, and when he had given thanks he broke it and gave it to his Apostles saying, 'This is my body, which is given unto you. Do this in memory of me.' And after they had eaten, he took the cup, saying, 'This wine that is

150

poured is the new covenant in my name, made for the forgiveness of sins.' How many have since tasted it and how few are really worthy! For he also said, 'I will drink no more of the fruit of the vine until I drink it with you again in my Father's kingdom.' Mark this, then, all of you, as you take this Holy Communion, as we taste his flesh and the Chosen sup of his real mortal blood.'

Lifting the chalice to the man's lips, he consecrates the cup, exchanging a few private words with the new initiate before removing his blindfold and leading him forward to begin a circuit of the room. Riding a wave of acclaim, the stag-priest shakes hands and gives blessings, liberally distributing one half of the sacrament and attending to the petitions of the parish whilst the others follow in his wake making the collection. In a few minutes his duty to most is done and the processional party are nearing me.

'Thank you for coming,' says one of the acolytes to the boy to my right. 'Can you spare something for the plate?'

He beams with pride as he donates a sixpence, his face falling as he is given the Host but passed over for the Cup.

'And how about you, sir?', the appeal directed at me.

Reluctantly, I shake my purse to see what small token I can afford.

'Wait!' intercedes the priest. 'What benighted pilgrim is this who deigns to darken my door?'

Before I can answer the new disciple is by his side.

'I know him!' he cries, hastily removing his holly crown and mane before kicking off his hoofs. It is none other than The Man of the River's querulous assistant who I left at Leicester Square. As I feel my eyes widen to mirror the manic expression in his, the priest says, 'Yes…and so do I,' taking off his own mask as standing before me is none other than the Irish Father and I wonder if all along I have been played like a fool on the infinite chessboard of old London town.

'Lord Almighty…'

'No,' he corrects me. 'Just a pale imitation,' his newly-restored voice still rich with Celtic mischief.'

'Father –'

'Do not use that word!'

'But…w-what has happened to you?' I stutter, quailing at the sight of cuts and bruises adorning his cheek and jaw.

'No worse than what happens to all nay-sayers. It is not every man who is prepared to pay the price of true faith,' lifting the disciple's shirt to reveal the results of the branding and rolling up his sleeve to display the same identical scar already seared into his wrist: the dove with flaming sword in its beak – clearly the emblem of his new 'church'.

Seeing my confusion, he takes my hand and I feel a lump of sentiment rising in my throat.

'It all started a way back, I forget exactly when: a nagging feeling that something was wrong. For years I kept my promise to him but rejoiced on the day I was finally set free – free, at last, to follow my own conscience. I had grown tired of my fellow clergy's lies and deceit; of their indulgence and craven pretence. In time, I came to see that they'd taken it from us and that we must move to take it back.'

'Take back what?' I ask him, bewildered.

'The Word, Jeremiah. The Word.'

At this, one of the acolytes steps forward. 'Here…eat of His body,' he says, offering me the holy bread.

I shake my head.

'Drink of His blood, then…'

'Never!' I refuse, setting my face like flint, unwilling to accept the tainted Eucharist.

'Jeremiah…' the priest warns me.

'No!' I cry. 'This Mass is surely blasphemy!'

'Alas, Jeremiah! You always had a good heart. Yet it can be quite a…revelation…when you read a well-thumbed text with a fresh new philosophy.'

'There is only one sacred text – and only one Word.'

'I know it well: soon this city will write and speak of nothing else.'

'Father! You have gone insane!'

'No, Jeremiah. I thought you knew your verse. Only those the Gods wish to destroy do they first make mad…'

152

I move to leave and the black flock are immediately upon me, a dozen followers at the behest of their chosen leader. Pinning me down, I struggle in vein against their number, my former teacher and protector calmly watching and waiting, unwavering in his conviction and stanch in his new mission.

'Let me go!' I implore them.

'Do not fight it, Jeremiah. Try to relax.'

'Father! Damien Patrick Cronin! Surely you of all people must see that this is wrong!'

'I see nothing and I am Damien Cronin no more. Did I not tell you, Master Carter, not to call me Father...'

He leans forward, pressing the Quaich to my lips, his eyes welling as a forest of fingers prize my mouth open and he tips a sickly warm liquid into the back of my throat.

'Now, be a good boy, and learn to take your medicine...'

Forcing me to gulp it down, he breathes a word into my ear - a four-lettered name charged with meaning and imbued with power without end - and my body turns to fire and my whole consciousness explodes as the sweet elixir hits my belly with instant effect. Rising from my back with the will of Lazarus, I see the chapters of my life existing all at once, many of the Chosen also poisoned by the preternatural potion running madly out of the tavern, sticks and bibles to hand. I, too, am borne with them on a surge of euphoria, dire Crusaders to a man, my last vision of the priest a small and shrunken figure fixed in front of the dancing flames like a flaking fresco of early sainthood.

Outside, on the fogged-gripped wharf, two fanatics lead the cause: a seaman and the artist's assistant.

'Hurry, Wat!' the sailor shouts, 'Let us do what must be done.'

Yet the lad ignores him, dropping back and vanishing into the murk as he goes his own way. Keen to follow, I turn to fetch the mare and bring the hansom with me. They are gone; all that remains a few links of iron chain hanging loosely from the inn's crumbling wall.

I call out her name and start to run, my imagination swarming with vague fears, struggling to keep my feet on the cobbles as I dash along the only gas-lit street. Passing rows of algae-covered buildings and pavements thick with slime, somewhere in the distance I think I hear a horse whinny and though I cannot be certain that it is Belle it is all the encouragement I need as I plunge deeper into the witches' brew.

I run, shouting her name.

'...Belle!...Belle!'

I listen for an answer but there is none.

I come to halt, hardly able to see my hand in front of my face.

I know not what to do, hope seems forlorn but she is out there somewhere and I must go on.

*

Here, in the shrouded square, Time stops and Day and Night have no dominion, the dripping walls and washed-out houses suspended in a grey netherworld like a story without title or end. I creep forward, keeping myself close to the brickwork, feeling my way along like a many-tentacled creature of the seabed, the only sound the needle-thin wheezing of my lungs as I try to grope a way through this unchartered creek with not a living soul to guide me...or is there?

A first clue to their presence: the faintest of whispers.

'Come, Jeremiah...find us...'

Halting, I listen: just silence, broken by the soft pitter-patter of water. Breathing in, I take a step forward.

'Over here, Jeremiah...'

I freeze. A child's voice, much clearer this time, no longer able to be dismissed as the tricks of an overwrought brain.

'Hide and seek, Jeremiah. You go first!'

'Over here!'

'No, not that way! Over here!'

I strive to peer through the veil but can make out nothing, now resolving to retrace my steps as quickly as I can. Assailed from all directions by teasing, pleading voices, blindly I go, the square filled with a deep moan of longing chased away by fits of callous laughter. Returning to what I believe to be the courtyard's entrance, I find the original ingress all bricked-up, my heart pounding and my head reeling as I lose all sense of order and direction as I twist about for any escape route.

In this, the loneliest hour before the dawn, all my failings must finally be faced in full and a heavy toll borne – and lo!, here it is, as out of the churning cauldron drops a series of Visions sent from Hell...

...an old man, head bowed and clothes clarted with muck hobbles through the fog, back bent with effort as he toils under the weight of something. I cough and he looks up – only then do I recognise Joseph Carter...'Ah! There you are, son! Not a moment too soon! I have been looking for your mother but I suppose you will be seeing her. I wished to say...would you tell her...I ought to have been a better husband...and I suppose, a better father.' He sighs and bites his lip as he stares at the ground. 'I did what I thought best at the time but now I see that I was wrong...I wanted everything for you, even though...'...He almost straightens and sniffs gratefully at the air. 'I have many calls upon me and much to do. Trouble not: all men have secrets - even men of God - and we all have our crosses to bear...' now shifting his load higher up his back as I see to my horror that he is carrying the trunk of a tree over his shoulder, yoked to its crossbar like an ox...

Before I have the chance to start after him or offer him solace the Vision fades and another follows in its wake...

...a foal gambols in a rich summer meadow with its mother, their delightful horseplay only interrupted by the rattle of the distant paddock gate. Two figures approach, calm and reassuring in manner, scattering a few grains of feed and gently haltering the mare. The foal looks right at me and I know that it is Belle – much younger than I ever knew her. Her ears prick up and a lasso is tossed around her neck and a hood thrown over her head, my ears tortured by her terrified whinnies and the cries of outrage of her struggling mother as she is roughly dragged away...

I cover my eyes, consumed by guilt and remorse, longing for respite but it is all no good…

…my fingers are prised open, the treachery of the field replaced by a homely scene: a woman in a bonnet sits in a rocking chair, softly singing to a babe cradled in her arms, her familiar profile - mother? - drawing me nearer to her until I can hear the words of her tender lullaby…'Rock-a-bye baby, on the treetop, when the wind blows, the cradle will rock…'…I edge round, her face hidden by her hat in the low light; she gets up, carrying the swaddling and approaching the glowing hearth…'If the bough breaks, the cradle will fall, but mother will catch you, cradle and all…' I make a lunge for the dark shape and grasp it in mid-air, pulling it to my chest then looking down to see not a helpless child of skin and bone but a dolly made of straw. As I drop it it falls into a puddle and she now caresses me, clucking like a watchful mother-hen. I touch her cheek and start to untie her bow, her healing hands now fixed around my throat like talons as her bonnet falls back to reveal puffy cheeks and two livid red eyes…

'ALICE!'

I choke under her iron grip but somehow fight back, struggling free and staggering forward into the fetid broth where I am greeted by a fresh chorus of hisses and howls, lurching on until I feel the air change and sense I have passed into an open space or a larger courtyard. My trial is not yet over though as before my eyes float a coterie of hard and haggard faces, making me reach in my pocket for the only set of verse which might just have the power to save me.

'Want the business, lover boy?' hiss a troika of banshees. 'We'll give you thrice a ride!'

'Father, can you hear my voice?' I cry. 'Have mercy, O God, according to your unfailing love…'

'Don't be shy!'

'Forget your precious filly!'

'I know that my sin is always before me. Against you, Lord, I have sinned and done what is evil in your sight…blot out my transgressions, wash away my iniquity…'

'Too late now!'

'Though I walk through the valley of the Shadow of Death, I will fear no Evil…'

They whine. 'And we fear no Psalm! Everyone knows the Revelations were given to John, not Jeremiah…'

My clammy fingers grasp something but instead of the Book I pull out the makeshift toeing knife, as I do so the women's wailing swallowed up by a deeper collective snarl.

A giant carousel of heads and ghastly cadavers, eyes rolling and tongues lolling, swoops down and spins around me like a visitation of Dread: convicts, mutineers and insane aristocrats, the profligate, dangerous and the Damned; Sirens waltzing with drowned and bloated admirals, palsied children, fallen tsars in tattered greatcoats and king's messengers cleft in two; nightwalkers, white walkers, mendicants in manacles, all chaperoned by a ring of swivelling skulls, impaled on their spikes at Traitors' Gate, hemming me in.

I slash wildly at the air in a bid for self-preservation, my skin crawling in the pungent presence of death, the heroic last stand of a cornered believer trapped in the Age of Progress. A few spatters of ghostly fluid sully my cape as my rips and tears make their mark and as a red mist descends my killing lust turns into a frenzy, every movement a mortal threat and all life anathema to me.

Above it all I hear a man speak: 'Will you?' he asks.

'Yes,' a woman replies.

Then, out of the fog comes a bloodcurdling scream and I hear a horse whinny again: louder, more persistent, snapping me out of my fever so that I drop my blunted blade and hurry with renewed purpose to trace both appeals to their source. Not so many streets away I find her: Belle, still strapped to the hansom, head lowered to the ground, nudging insistently at what looks to be a bundle of rags. As I approach the disordered heap I notice it is sodden with what I first take to be water; then, in the half-light, I see the dark

157

pool growing and spreading across the cobbles, stooping down to examine the still and crumpled form to behold nothing short of an abomination: a woman's remains, more offal than human, lie with legs splayed and clothes disarranged, its crimson wounds and many hurts defying all reasonable description, gutted like a pig at market. In her hand she still clutches a piece of lace and her glassy eyes gaze up into the forever and if I did not know her at first then I do now, for she was the fare I abandoned in Whitechapel's rain.

Still warm to the touch, I find two penny pieces and gently close her eyelids, her head falling to one side and nearly rolling away as I sicken at the sight of the fatal cut, more the work of a devil than a man – product of a deranged mind or a wracked and blackened soul.

Dazed with horror, I mumble incoherently for help, to be quietened by the fall of heavy hoofs that do not belong to Belle. Out of the vapour a manservant appears holding a flare, lighting the way for a most ornate carriage. Dressed in full funeral attire, he is outdone only by the raven plumes of its four black stallions, feisty and maleficent thoroughbreds all who nonetheless answer to their master's silent bidding as the driver pulls up, throwing the reins upon their backs and without need of clear signal or harsh instruction has the terrible quartet held in abeyance.

Leaping onto the cobbles he walks towards me and I whimper at the jangle of his spurs and the brush of his cloak…but it is not me he wants as he reaches down to claim his quarry, plucking the woman's body from the ground as though she were a feather, carrying her to the waiting gig. A vice-like cold seems to seep not in but out of the cracks of its doors and blacked-out windows, what little light there is picking out only its overpainted coat-of-arms. Flinging her in, the coachman climbs up to retake the reins and as the Four bear her away on her last earthly journey my fear turns to envy as I watch the spectral cortege withdraw, yearning to catch it up so that I may hitch a ride, and, having bested the bounce of its springs and revolution of its wheels, clamber inside as I look to split the bill, knowing only too well the price of a rider's favours and the long wait in store for those left at the rank.

159

11

Four Horsemen

AS DAWN RISES I stir as if from a dream as the hansom splashes its way through the rutted streets, happy to let the grey follow her nose as we turn our backs on Mother Thames and leave the madness of night behind us.

Birdsong pierces the air, fear and evil flee and even the highways seem to shimmer, the earlier deluge having washed away much of the mire as the great and sovereign city awakens. In Billingsgate and Broadway marts will soon open and traders ready themselves for business, as in the elegant town houses of Brompton and Westminster maids polish their grates and set kitchen fires; in Greenwich half the civilized world's routine rests on the tick of a single clock, and even in Brent and distant Cockfosters where London exists only as a rumour, news will arrive with the morning mail of all the vanity, drama, hysteria and pathos that only a legend in the making can possibly inspire.

Five million of the citizenry will draw their swords and prepare to do good battle but as the nation's capital comes to life I can think only of my bed, the straight road south my own 'noblest prospect' as I look out for the first of Bermondsey's spires that speak to my heart of homestead and rest, returning for but a few hours' kind repose.

Having bid goodbye to the docklands we make steady progress as Hickman's Folly's islands of weeds and the railway arches of Spa Road give way to semi-respectable blocks: pathways widen, porticoes seem not so rueful, masonry tarnished not with years of accumulated soot but patches of silver lichen. High above me a skylark sings and soars, lifting my jaded spirit with it, bringing me hope that somewhere we might still find:

'Tongues in trees, books in running brooks, sermons in stones and good in everything.'

Fine sentiments, however, I have come to realize, are not enough on their own as even the improving vistas and purer air cannot banish my native doubts and misgivings over this latest atrocity I have witnessed.

In the burgeoning sunlight rats scatter as images from the night creep back into my thoughts like late or uninvited guests, cast with a newer tint. It began with the bailie, my dealings with him a lifetime ago so now it seems. Domineering and puffed-up as he was from the outset, his pompous rhetoric and haughty manner indicated to one who has met many a real peer more than a few chinks in his imperious ego, his nervousness and excitement in my presence masked by a raft of petty questions. I do not disbelieve that he was in need of a ride and remarkable indeed was the view we both enjoyed of the illuminated Thames – yet how necessary was it that he actually disembark and what, I wonder, was he hoping to incite in his prying ways or in his two-minute stint on the knoll of the dusky common?

Next, Covent Garden, and the jovial lad who earned his shilling as I wet my beak and took my evening bite. Innocence incarnate, as honest as the day is long: this whelp who lives on his wits and whatever poor sustenance his irregular gains may afford him. No ordinary street Arab he, who, not just content to pass the time of day to pave the way to modest riches, revelled in the chance to quote arcane scripture in demonstration of his own beliefs. His knowledge, though, and his extreme attachment to the teachings will be his own undoing, instilling in him a fatal honesty that leaves his innermost thoughts exposed. Did he recite his Apocalyptic verse to please or appease me – and why exactly would a fellow believer be afraid of a ghost, less still a visiting angel?

Why did my man MacIver feign drunkenness and sleep before his reckless dead-of-night flit, knowing, surely, that a quibble over money is better resolved by negotiation than by flight? And why, oh why, did the woman who sought my services then make me

161

leave her in the lurch, still later heading to the docks as I stupidly advised?

For the question I really ask here is not what do I see in them but what do they see in me, for of the many fares I dropped off and collected none was more lost than I. Bolstered by liquor, in need of society or in search of sweet release, only the barmy and bereft freely climbed into my cab, their fear gone, knowing me for what I am.

And then, of course, there is the small matter of Belle.

*

Many of the professions are kind of a brotherhood, men with a deep-felt sense of association, resulting in co-operatives and members clubs based solely on a shared livelihood. Surgeons have their halls, quilters their guilds, even Oddfellows meet to sup; scattered places - some resplendent, others less so - for otherwise strangers to come together, learn, improve and take stock. Not so, for the humble cab driver.

Though there may be in excess of ten thousand of us patrolling the streets at any one time and much as commerce, Parliament and Empire would grind to a halt without our faithful service, it is a fact that our particular line of work is isolating by its very nature, fostering secrecy, suspicion, and above all silence, and giving rise to a mutual but unwritten creed extending far beyond our hours of toil to at all times cover our ears, close our eyes, stay our hands and keep our counsel. Nowhere will you find a carriage driver's union, a groomsman's league or horseman's house, the Cabman's Shelter his closest thing to a masonic temple – and in the rare places where we do sometimes meet, we meet in stealth and under pain of death.

With beasts, not people, is how we chiefly spend our time, for we tend to be sullen, cagey, hard to pin down and undesiring of the ties of friendship; mares make no big demands and colts are less gregarious than even ourselves, our irreproachable understanding a strange but perfect marriage of common need and likeminded sorts.

162

Family and faith is all the fraternity we have; when either or both fail or flounder our coaches hit the dirt and our cabs veer off the tracks.

*

I leave Belle at the gate by the long and dewy grass, not even bothering to tie her up this time, knowing she will still be there when I return. Here, in the final resting place of my ancestors, I can at last find a little peace.

A three-quarter acre plot tucked between the Sunday school and the road to the public baths, Boutcher Cemetery has for two hundred years provided dignity to the dead and succour to the mourning, its long-term residents afforded a good night's rest and a standard of dying way beyond anything they dreamed of during their stunted lives. Yet despite its modest size and orderly appearance, I am reliably informed by one of its custodians that in places its coffins are stacked ten or eleven stories deep making it one of Southwark's largest burial grounds, a vast necropolis of nameless thousands bursting at the seams under the strain of its rotting roll as first Bermondsey, then London and finally all of England itself slowly turns into one enormous grave.

Today, any incomer with no local connections will struggle to secure a spot but at least I do not have to suffer such worries as I make my way to the north-west corner to visit my family's tomb.

As I near it I feel myself stiffen for I regret to say that ours is not one of the prettiest; as the last living descendant the responsibility to tend it is mine and mine alone, and, as I have not paid my respects recently and have developed an aversion to fresh blooms for reasons I hardly need explain, I find it cheerless and reproving, the carvings crumbling and the oldest inscriptions already weathering, the once-neat edging rank with brambles and overgrown with willow herb as Nature pays her own tribute.

Yet still, beneath the listing headstone, are interred three generations of Carters.

First, the hand-chiselled legend:

163

Here Lieth
JOSIAH MATTHEW CARTER
Husband of Agnes and beloved father to Joseph.
Born 26th November, 1809
Died 5th March, 1868
"Christ will gather in His own."

Immediately below, the sharper for being newer:

Also
JOSEPH ISIAH CARTER
Ever devoted to his wife Jean and His son Jeremiah.
Born 10th January, 1828
Died 2nd July, 1883
"I sought the Lord and He heard me."

And thirdly...but wait a moment, for I know I just told you that three were interred here when perhaps I ought to have said 'remembered'. For the last tribute, flawless as if just inscribed, reads:

Also
J CARTER
"Awake, arise or be forever fall'n."

No: not I, for as far as I am aware I am not dead yet. 'Who, then?' you rightly ask.

Burdensome duty of mine it is to now tell you the full tale of my grievous loss. Hark – for you know something already and have heard a true account of my Fall that bleak and cruel midwinter's night. You know of snow, hail, wind and ice, and a man's foolish greed that kept him from his gate. You know of an ailing wife left alone in her sick room, frightened, fretful and dry with thirst. You know of a message sent and received too late. You know of panic, repentance and a love forever cursed. Yet still, within this bitter truth, there was something I neglected to tell you.

For in that dynasty of horsemen there was a fourth, for when she died Alice was with child. He - for a boy it was to be - perished in the womb of his mother: our much wanted son, to be called John, known as Jack.

Now that I have told you I feel as if a great weight has been lifted from my shoulders and perhaps, after all, it is for the best that I stand here as the end of this once proud and hale but now failed and corrupted line; gone they may be, but my flesh and blood speak clearest to me here and I hear every word they say.

I raise my head and shiver, ready to turn away, when an arc of colour catches my eye: the memorial, ever drab, is lit by the rays of the rising sun and crowned by a brilliant pink halo. Amazed, I move closer, to see that the limestone is garlanded with tiny, impeccable stars; can it be possible - nay! – and yet I see it clearly - for there can be no real doubt of her presence here and that this, set amongst the dead, is her loudest living sign.

Kneeling, I see that the ladder of perfect flowers climb up the headstone's rim from a small gap in the grass where the border meets the grave's kerb; brushing away the loose soil, I pull and claw at the turf, convinced now that I have found the way to them both and prepared to dig for as long as it takes to heave them back into the light. I tear away, happy as a clam at high water, unmindful of the setting or hour, when a harsh squawk rips me out of my reverie and I catch myself, nails black with dirt and eyes trained on the hollow ground like a hunting dog at earth, as a lone crow perched on the wall watches my strange performance, hopeful of a chance of food.

I sit up with a start, wipe my fingers on the grass then struggle to my feet. Abashed, I clap my hands at the bird who takes to the wing and caws his discontent, as I hastily stamp down the sod and brush the loam off my breeks. Not wishing to linger or even offer a parting prayer to the memory of my antecedents, I make for the ivy-covered gates, knowing that my place here will be kept forever warm for me as the crushed, unmissed and dearly departed face the fickle fate of morning together.

*

Like Paul on the final stretch of the road to Damascus, I approach Peter's Yard as a man with vision blurred but with God and revelation near.

In the low sunlight I can just about make out my plucky grey, limping but valiantly pulling us home, no doubt even keener than I to see an end to her labours. My love for her swamps me like a spring tide, haunted by the memory of what she once was - of what we both were - and it occurs to me as it so often has before that it is the mares of this world who are the source of half of our joy and the cause of nearly all our pain.

I wonder how much longer she can go on – but old and worn as she is, and blind as I may be, I see that it is she, more than any, who holds the key.

Much as Alice brought me hope and forgiveness through her floral magic so does Belle bring me truth, for animals do not lie. Whilst we men are masters of ruse and deception as we relentlessly pursue our own ends, a horse like Belle is incapable of disguising her emotions even to her disadvantage or risk of her own life. She - like dozens more stabled at the Yard - has indeed been behaving mightily strangely of late – and no stranger than tonight.

Take, for example, this sudden lameness without a cause, flaring up with no warning and at various stages of the night before righting itself seemingly at will and then not recurring for many a wearisome shift. Tonight, it appeared as we took the flat City road to Whitechapel – where next, I wonder: at dusk tomorrow by St Martin-in-the-Fields or on the stroke of midnight the day after as we pass Horse Guards Parade? Then, there is this business of halting and refusing to work, a trait I have never previously observed in a well-trained mount, not least one such as Belle, injury or no. Her wild foaming at the mouth at Smithfield; her later insistence that I walk by her side and, worst of all, her out of character wanderlust in the dirty heart of the docklands' dark: what common denominator possibly united aberrations such as these?

Yet the more I dwell, the less do such recollections tally with my earlier perceptions of the night. Subtle and sensitive beast she may be but serial shirker she is not; she limps, then, if not in discomfort or pain, but to send out a warning. Furthermore, all horses, cabmen know, will foam at mouth during any prolonged exercise; but what can be a sign of perfect health in some can, with cold sweat and pupils wide, speak of a beast not high in the heat of exertion but intoxicated by pure fear. Triggered, perhaps, by the scent of blood, a normal lather quickly becomes a deadly drooling so that a bridled mare can hardly breathe. More relaxed she certainly was later on with me down and walking by her side but for the first time I think I start to see the real reason why…and as for her disappearing act – what I had initially feared to be the work of horse rustlers, then put down to a fit of nerves has now taken on a deeper shape and meaning, for the Belle I know would never consent to leave with a stranger without putting up a fight and for her to abscond and therefore abandon her master there must have been something - or someone - for her to need to escape from.

Was this the wall foretold by the Oracle of my youth or the evil destiny from which the Lascar's amulet could still perhaps protect me? Pulling it out of my shirt I find that it bends like putty in my hand; what I took to be real silver just some cheap base metal not able to even protect itself from the bodily heat that has somehow caused it to melt. As we pass the tall white tower of St Mary Magdalen's I wrench it from my neck in scorn, consigning the false idol - and with it all of the acts and episodes of the night - into the waiting gutter.

*

Peter's Yard is already lively on our return; not wishing to be waylaid, I drive the cab straight into its station and, unhitching Belle, lead her to the wash bay outside her stall, removing her headgear, rubbing her down and wiping away the blood, sweat and grime. Thing of hoof and hair as she is, she is as much a child of mine as he that I lost – he that, God-willing, 'though his grave be England, his dying place is Paradise'.

Yet from the depths of my Fall I have come to see that human life is full of such trials, misfortunes and disappointments, and what is a man to do but honestly face them, striving in his own small way, as I have done, to realign the stars.

Do you wish to me to say more? I will not. For I have already said too much and laboured long whilst other men slept. I leave it to others to justify the ways of a man to God, more still of gods to men.

My tired grey is impatient to be let her into her stall, but exhausted as she is, she keeps her eyes trained on me until I step outside and bolt the stable door. Leaving her be, I make one final check of my cab, suddenly remembering the Gladstone bag; reaching up, I open it and hurriedly stuff it with rags, stowing it back under the seat from where it came, vowing to deal with it later at a more convenient time. For now, this hansom may well be working a double-tide, in which case it will need an hour's attention before heading back out onto the road. The affairs of day, however, are no longer my concern so I soon slip across the busy yard and as I pass through the gates and out onto the cobbles a cock crows, the church bells ring and I know that my night's work is done.

Afterword

New Year's Day is not a time I readily associate with *Cripps* – or any aspect of work.

In the normal course of events, like millions of others, I would be nursing a major hangover or else lounging around at home wondering how long I might keep those ill-advised resolutions. That particular January 1st, however, had not been a normal one and though I had certainly had my share of booze and delicious party food both before and after the fireworks and bells, it had, for once, not been taken alone in my flat in front of the TV next to the three bar fire but rather in the company of dozens of others – young, charming and indeed beautiful people who not only seemed eager to court my company but were desperate to keep my champagne flute well topped-up and spoil me with a variety of canapés.

In between rubbing shoulders with famous writers and publishers and introductions to agents who hovered like vultures, I had been pulled aside to give a couple of radio interviews, now much more at ease with being put on the spot and certainly better-practised at the art of saying nothing too offensive, in the end managing to slip away and hail a taxi to Whitechapel so that I could escape to the relative sanctuary of the shop.

It had hardly been two months since the publication of the book yet as I looked at the growing pile of mail on the counter, I knew I had hundreds of orders and inquiries to catch up on that could no longer be ignored, feeling that (much like grandpa Cornelius back in the day) I would soon have no choice but to employ an industrious assistant to allow me the liberty of an occasional day off and the luxury of reflecting upon where I had once been and the alien place I seemed to be heading so rapidly to.

None of this had yet made its way into the consciousness of my small circle of acquaintances and friends to whom I must have appeared to be struggling manfully on in an enterprise with precious little going for it and which, more likely than not, would fade into oblivion with my own inevitable passing. I preferred it this way, dreading the time when my success (such as it was) and the money it would bring might irrevocably alter the nature of our friendships.

Much of the early interest that the book had generated had come from across the Pond, prompted by what I had thought to be a low-key article in a south Delaware weekly, and by a process of word of mouth this excitement and enthusiasm had spread around the globe as I received messages, fan mail and more formal correspondence not merely in relation to Carter's story but also the general contents of my shop, so that I soon sold out of all items salvaged from the life of the old East End, the world of horses, carts and hansom cabs – just about everything, in fact, with the most tenuous link to what is now fashionably called 'Victoriana'. As such, when I was rudely awoken a few hours later by the high-pitched ring of the telephone, I reached up to drag the old Bakelite handset closer to me and immediately recognised the now familiar click and crackle of an international call.

'*Cripps*…Yes?'

'Happy New Year, Mr Julian.'

'Rami?' I asked blearily. 'Is that you?'

'But of course. Who else?'

'Where are you?'

'I am here in glorious Dhaka visiting distant relations. I did tell you I was going.'

'Oh…yes, I remember now.' I pressed the light on my watch. 'You do know it's six o'clock in the morning here, don't you?'

'Is it really? I had forgot. Here it is midday – and the temperature is nearly thirty degrees.'

'Lucky you. It's bloody Baltic here and I can see my own breath.'

'How awful. You really should come for a visit. Step out of London. Spread your wings.'

174

'Hm. Yes, well I'd like to but –'

'Yes yes: I know. You have no time. Your business. The money. But we only live once you know – and I say that as a born-again Hindu.'

'Very funny. Well, perhaps I might just do it one day.'

'Wonderful! I can always help you if you wish. May I also ask why you are at work on a Bank Holiday? I did try you at home first.'

'Oh…I just have a few things I need to do,' I replied vaguely, somehow reluctant to share with him the happy news of the last fortnight's startling turn of events.

'How is the shop doing?' he continued.

'Fair to middling,' I lied.

'Many customers?'

'One or two.'

'I take it you mean that literally. Have you given any more thought to the offer I made you?'

'I must admit,' I told him, 'that I have.'

'And?'

'Let's discuss it face-to-face. I'll wait till you get back.'

'I understand. There is no rush here. We must do things properly. I look forward to hearing what you have to say. Ah! It looks like my lunch is ready. I must go. I hope that you enjoy the rest of your day.'

'Thank you. I'm sure I will.'

'Goodbye Mr Julian.'

'Goodbye Rami. Oh…and Rami?'

'Yes?'

'Happy New Year.'

He rang off. I couldn't help but smile: the New Year was barely a few hours old and yet here was Rami Mistry already conscientiously attending to business – probably why he was an infinitely better entrepreneur than I…or at least, why he *had* been. I wondered what he would make of the new incarnation of Julian Cripps: writer, historian, publisher…star. How would he take to fielding inane, repetitive questions about his long-time and suddenly celebrated neighbour? How would he feel about a procession of fraught couriers asking *him* to take in yet another cumbersome delivery of packages and mail, the shutters of *Cripps* drawn once again as its absentee owner fulfilled whatever obligations his new-found status seemed to demand of him on a near daily basis? And, perhaps most importantly, how would he react as it dawned on him that his long-held ambitions for my enviably-situated shop unit were now little more than a pipe dream?

Ho-hum. Such is life and I had no doubt at all that in time Rami would get over the minor disappointment and his budding empire go from strength to strength. But this was *my* time now – and also that of *Cripps*: the culmination of seven turbulent decades of hope, discovery, disaster and renewal; against all odds we had made the mountain top, all the stronger for that which had not destroyed us, eager to plant our flag in virgin soil and lay claim to our rightful part of the expedition's spoils.

In such a spirit I got to my feet, tired but determined to seize the day in a year when all would run to the Julian calendar. I stopped. A collision of disparate thoughts: New Year's Day; last night's fireworks over the Thames; the fluctuating fortunes of the family business; my high hopes for the coming year. I flicked on the light and checked under the counter. Still there: the battered old Gladstone and inside, now protected by a sturdy box, the carefully restored journal. What was the ancient ritual again? To make one's way to the nearest bridge and to throw something in by way of tribute, in return for a prosperous year. I grabbed my coat, put on a hat, scarf and gloves, and, taking the bag and journal with me, exited the shop, heading south along Brick Lane in the biting January cold.

In my haste to make my pilgrimage it took a few moments for me to realize that something was amiss: in both directions, the entire length of the Curry Mile sat in total darkness bar the solitary light in the main foyer of my shop. No lamppost, street light or restaurant sign penetrated the last hour of night, the result being that for the first time in as long as I could remember I could actually see stars, constellations and even the Milky Way painted

176

across the forgotten canvass high above Central London, with one cluster in particular - was it Pegasus? No doubt Carter could have told me - shining brightly just over the horizon.

As I turned onto Whitechapel Road, then Mansell Street it was worth it just to walk the deserted streets, strewn as they were with the remains of a night's wild celebrations all picked over by a lone rubbish collector who seemed unfazed by the gargantuan scale of his task. Very soon the unmistakable silhouette of Tower Bridge - and then the beckoning dark ribbon of the great river herself - loomed into view, sobering me up a little and prompting me to slow my pace to review the wisdom of my plan. In the form of the Gladstone bag and the now notorious journal I had certainly brought something valuable with me, for which I could already make a pretty penny as I rode the crest of the book's growing fame – yet this was one sale that *Cripps ABC* was not willing to make.

I'd already had a brief taste of the shape of things to come in which I'd found myself beset with offers and inquiries. In a few cases, the passionate interest which my version of Carter's story had stirred had crossed the line from innocent fandom into intrusive and wholly inappropriate demands for personal photos, confidential information and the like. One gentleman in particular had begun to bother me, his initial polite questions rapidly escalating into repeated requests for my qualifications and credentials, and now (I feared, if I did not nip things in the bud) threatening to turn into a malicious daily campaign of bullying and harassment demanding access to what was, I could hardly deny, much more than just an old diary but in fact a rare historical document.

No: I'd soon decided that I would rather see the thing destroyed than let it fall into another's hands. The river was the best and natural place for it, for having given she would always gratefully receive, swallowing the Gladstone whole and dispersing its contents at her own divine will. Making the crossing, I found it still cordoned off with a line of temporary metal fencing but with no-one in sight I clambered over and continued on to the middle point, putting the bag down and peering over the parapet. Immediately the bridge burst into life, lit up like a giant Christmas tree, with flashing blues and wailing sirens racing towards me, followed by the heavy screeching of tyres.

'Don't move! Stay exactly where you are!' barked a voice through a distant loudhailer.

Bemused, I waved my hands in apology and began to edge away.

'I said, 'DON'T MOVE'!'

I saw the shape of two policemen step out of the car, cautiously approaching as the voice addressed me from somewhere high within the structure of the bridge.

'Put your hands behind your head! Now turn around.'

'Is everything alright, sir?' one of the officers asked me, and as I was about to reply I felt one of them make a grab for my arm, yanking me down in one swift movement as I crumpled onto the icy pavement. In a few seconds I found myself in handcuffs and was soon subjected to the indignity of a police check.

Morning had broken before they were finally happy to release me, issuing me with a caution and reuniting me with the bag and journal but only after they had given both the full treatment. I limped back to Whitechapel, vowing for now to stow the Gladstone in the securest place possible: my shop safe which also contained several items of costume jewellery handed down to me by my father, their royal connections making them the most valuable set in my possession and representing my retirement fund. As I neared the shop, though, I saw a few figures loitering outside, pointing and taking photographs. I froze with guilt. Not the Press already, surely? Fortunately not, for as I neared I saw it was a group of late revellers, so I waited until I was sure they had gone.

Relieved to be back in one piece, I quickly locked the bag away and returned the counter. Then I saw it: a single slip of paper, marooned in the dust-free island in the spot where the telephone had long sat. I reached over, picked it up and instantly knew the red script: the wilder version, written on headed bill-paper, bespattered with old mud and marked with a dirty thumbprint, entirely fitting to the grim setting in which it appeared to have been transcribed.

As I looked the words over, I felt a shiver run through me and the hairs stand up on the back of my neck; an overreaction, perhaps, in the cold confines of the shop but one which I cannot yet seem to shake. I fear that this whole strange affair is finally catching up with me and that I indeed need to get away to warmer climes. Thus, I leave it to you, my wise readers, to decide for yourselves whether what I read forms a simple set of instructions – or else a radical new turn at poetry by one whose adventures have led us this far and who desired, when left alone in the everlasting twilight, nothing more than to improve his chosen art…

MURPHY'S
136 The Highway, Limehouse.

"The Gralloch"

Hack, slice, tear, rip.
Insert blade above the breast.
Work around so blood flows freely,
kneel on ribs to drain the chest.

Cut the throat and tie the food-pipe
so as not to spoil the meat.
Open stomach, pull out gralloch,
leave the pluck, leave the feet.

Check for foetus deep inside,
puncture not its sacred sack.
Inspect carcass for disease
now it's lifeless on its back.

Hide for leather and flesh for cat food,
blood for compost, feet for glue.
Not for her a Christian burial,
thank the Lord it isn't you.

Bones for oil and hair for cushions,
naught is wasted; do not be vexed.
Lo! Do I see another patron?
Sharpen your knife and onto the next!

J.C.

VERSE

In his musings, Jeremiah Carter quotes from the following works:

Paradise Lost, by John MILTON, first published by Samuel Simmons, London, 1667.

The Lotos-Eaters by Alfred TENNYSON, first published by Edward Moxon, London, 1832.

The Tempest and *As You Like It,* by William SHAKESPEARE, first published by William and Isaac Jaggard and Edward Blount, London, 1623.

The Faerie Queene, by Edmund SPENSER, first published by William Ponsonbie, London, 1590.

I See The Four-Fold Man, from *Jerusalem*, by William BLAKE, first printed by William Blake, London, 1804-1820.

A Hymn For Christmas Day, by Thomas CHATTERTON, written in London, 1764. First publication date unknown.

Religio Medici, by Thomas BROWNE, first published by Andrew Crooke, London, 1642.

AND

The King James Bible, first published by Robert Barker, London, 1611.

Acknowledgements

The author would like to thank the following people,
who,
knowingly and unknowingly,
helped with the writing of this book:
Lydia Horsman, Kerry Fogarty and
Ben Naismith.

Also my parents Jean and Paul, and my sister Lucy,
beloved Bob, Bobby and Charlie,
All of my family and friends
And the Scottish Gang.

In particular,
I want to thank my Best Man, Robert Chamberlain for years
of priceless friendship
And
Daniele Serra for his incredible vision.

I am deeply indebted to Mr Julian Thorley and
Dr Timothy Mellor of Regensburg
who kindly read earlier drafts of this book
and whose detailed feedback
helped to make 'Carter' a much better book.

I am also grateful to my aunt Sue Virgo
for her extensive research on our family history
which helped to inspire and inform certain aspects of
'Carter'.

Lastly,
I wish to thank my beloved wife Christine for her love, loyalty and wisdom,
and who,
in the face of every evidence to the contrary,
never stopped believing.

This Book

is dedicated to my beloved wife Christine

and

to all the horses who ever worked on the streets of

old London town.